THE MEN OF
BITTER CREEK

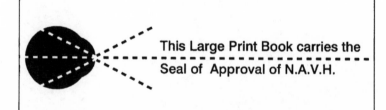

This Large Print Book carries the
Seal of Approval of N.A.V.H.

THE MEN OF BITTER CREEK

(Originally published in <u>To Have and to Hold</u> and <u>A Christmas Together</u>)

Joan Johnston

Published in 2005 by arrangement with Avon Books,
an imprint of HarperCollins Publishers Inc.

Wheeler Large Print Hardcover.

The text of this Large Print edition is unabridged.
Other aspects of the book may vary from the original edition.

Set in 16 pt. Plantin by Minnie B. Raven.

Printed in the United States on permanent paper.

Library of Congress Cataloging-in-Publication Data

Johnston, Joan, 1948–
    [Man from Wolf Creek]
    The Men of Bitter Creek / by Joan Johnston.
        p. cm.
    ISBN 1-58724-953-7 (lg. print : hc : alk. paper)
    1. Large type books.   I. Johnston, Joan, 1948–
Christmas baby.   II. Title.
PS3560.O3896M36 2005
813'.54—dc22   2005000141

THE MEN OF
BITTER CREEK

As the Founder/CEO of NAVH, the only national health agency solely devoted to those who, although not totally blind, have an eye disease which could lead to serious visual impairment, I am pleased to recognize Thorndike Press* as one of the leading publishers in the large print field.

Founded in 1954 in San Francisco to prepare large print textbooks for partially seeing children, NAVH became the pioneer and standard setting agency in the preparation of large type.

Today, those publishers who meet our standards carry the prestigious "Seal of Approval" indicating high quality large print. We are delighted that Thorndike Press is one of the publishers whose titles meet these standards. We are also pleased to recognize the significant contribution Thorndike Press is making in this important and growing field.

Lorraine H. Marchi, L.H.D.
Founder/CEO
NAVH

* Thorndike Press encompasses the following imprints: Thorndike, Wheeler, Walker and Large Print Press.

Contents

The Man
from
Wolf Creek

One

Cale shivered in his buckskins as he pulled the bearskin coat tighter around his chin to fend off the sting of blowing snow. He hadn't precisely expected this spring blizzard, but he had lived in the Teton Mountains long enough to plan ahead for the unpredictable weather. There was no one to save him if he got into trouble. He was on his own in this lonesome wilderness. It was a choice he had made ten years ago, when he was twenty-four. He had never regretted his decision to leave the civilized world behind.

Cale had checked most of his traps before the storm hit and had already started back to his cabin while the snow was still falling in flakes that slowly, gently buried the June flora. Now the wind whistled down the back of his neck, and the snow was deep enough to slip into his knee-length moccasins and melt around his toes. Best he could figure, he had another half mile of uphill walking to do before he could settle down in front of a roaring fire and wait out the storm.

The sight of a saddled mule sitting on its haunches between two lodgepole pines stopped him in his tracks. Cale shook his head in disgust when he saw the figure of a man yanking on the mule's bridle, trying to get the animal on its feet. The man wasn't wearing a coat, and despite his slouch hat, his eyebrows and mustache were white with snow. Cale considered making a detour around man and mule, but another look at the flannel shirt and denim trousers the old man wore convinced him the idiot would freeze to death if left on his own.

"Need some help?" Cale asked as he stepped into the stranger's line of vision.

The man let the reins drop and turned to face Cale. His eyes crinkled with pleasure, and he shoved his hat back and brushed the snow from his mustache with two quick flips of his wrist. "Glory be! Figured I was gonna freeze to death for sure. Didn't look like snow when I left the valley this morning." He held out his hand. "Name's Orrin Schuyler. You got a cabin somewheres close? I'm about to freeze my arse off."

Cale grimaced and ignored the outstretched hand. "About a half mile up. Follow me."

"Why, I'd surely like to do that, son, but Betsy here, she ain't moving. Can't leave her here. The two of us have been together a long time."

Cale walked over to the animal, murmured a few words into the mule's ear, turned his back and began walking away. Betsy brayed once as she struggled to her feet and followed docilely after him.

Orrin gathered up the reins and hurried after Cale. "I'll be hornswoggled. What did you say to her?"

"That if she stayed where she was, some Blackfoot or Arikara would have her for supper."

Orrin guffawed and slapped his knee. "Guess you told her, all right. Didn't catch your name, son."

Cale gave Orrin a cold stare. "I'm not your son, old man."

"No offense meant," Orrin said with a hop-skip through the deep snow to catch up with Cale's longer strides. "So what are you called, boy?"

Cale frowned ferociously at the old man. *Boy* wasn't much of an improvement over *son*. Being alone so much, Cale wasn't used to talking. He found the old man's questions irritating. But Orrin Schuyler looked stubborn enough to keep yammering until he got an answer, so Cale said, "Name's Cale Landry."

"Cale Landry," Orrin murmured. "Heard tell of you at the last rendezvous down in Willow Valley. You the one can shoot the eye from a turkey at two hundred paces?" Without waiting for an answer Orrin continued, "Heard you don't come down from the mountains much, but when you do, you got the finest beaver pelts a body's ever seen. Story is some Flathead Injun woman taught you how to cure them skins so nice and purty. That so, boy? You an Injun lover?"

Orrin chuckled deep in his throat. "Guess folks'd call me an Injun lover too, seein's how I got me a daughter by one of them squaws. The girl's ma was one of them Nez Perce Injuns. Always stood so tall and straight, like she was some kinda queen, when she wasn't no such thing. Made you feel like you oughtta bow down to her. Raven — that's my daughter — turned out the same way. That girl fairly oozes pride."

Orrin clucked his tongue. "Her ma was some woman, all right. Died 'fore I learned the secret from her of how to cure skins so

14

nice. Didn't seem no need for it while she was alive, and once she was dead, well, it was too late then. You're a lucky man, Cale Landry."

Right then, Cale was regretting the impulse that had led him to save the talkative old man. He caught sight of his cabin through the blowing snow and heaved a sigh of relief. Which turned out to be premature. Once the old man was warmed up, his lips loosened even more.

" 'Preciate you putting Betsy in the lean-to with your horse. Mighty fine bunch of furs you got stored in there, Cale. You must've had a right fine winter of trapping. Beaver and marten and muskrat, all three. Me, I ain't been doin' so well lately." The old man pulled a deck of worn cards from his vest pocket and shuffled them in his hands. "Wasn't for my girl selling buckskins with fancy Injun beadwork, we'd'a gone hungry once or twice this past winter. Figured I'd hunt us up some venison for supper tonight. Woulda had a fine buck too, hadn't been for this blizzard."

Cale went on with his regular routine, gutting and cleaning the rabbits he had caught and making a stew from them. He did his best to avoid Orrin, who wandered around the small room shuffling his cards.

15

Cale hoped the snow would stop by morning. He didn't want to put the old man out in the storm, but he had learned that when it came to survival, a man had to do what a man had to do. He wouldn't last another day with Orrin Schuyler yakking away in his cabin.

"Nice place you got here." Orrin slapped his deck of cards on the trestle table that dominated the center of the room. "Mighty comfortable. That pine bed of yours looks big enough to share."

"You sleep in front of the fire." Cale pointed to the huge buffalo robe he had put down to keep the drafts from seeping in under the wooden floor of the cabin. He didn't intend to knock elbows with the other man in bed. But he had a feeling it wasn't going to be easy to ignore Orrin Schuyler's presence. With his luck, the old man probably snored.

Cale turned a deaf ear to Orrin's chatter and surveyed his domain. The log walls were well chinked with a mixture of mud and grass, and the single window was covered with an animal skin scraped thin enough to let in a shadowy light. The door hung on leather hinges, and he had used strips of buckskin to seal it around the edges. Several kerosene lanterns provided

16

light to work by. It was an extravagance he allowed himself, like the books he bought. After all, there wasn't much else he could do with his earnings, living alone like he did.

Maybe the place was a little cluttered, but that was one advantage of living alone. He knew where everything was, because there was no one to move things around. And maybe he didn't clean as often as he should, but there was no one he had to impress. It stunk a little, but that was the natural result of his trade. He worked outside as much as he could because the cabin was too small to be truly comfortable for a man his size. Adding a second person had made it downright crowded.

"Do you suppose it's snowing down in the valley, too?" Orrin asked. "Or just up here? Hope that girl of mine has sense enough to find some shelter."

"You don't have a cabin?" Cale asked.

"Naw. Been camping out under the stars, waiting for everyone to show up for the rendezvous next month in Pierre's Hole. Figured to bunk in a tent with some friends of mine."

"How old is your girl?" Cale asked, suddenly alarmed at the thought of a child left all alone in the storm.

"Be nineteen this summer. Believe me, Raven can take care of herself. She's got gumption, all right. Just ain't been tapped yet. Little bit shy, is all. Don't cotton much to white folks. Which ain't surprising, considering she's half Injun."

Cale had seen how capable an Indian woman could be on her own, but he wondered how much this white man's daughter knew of the Indian ways. "How old was Raven when her mother died?"

" 'Bout six, I guess. She lived with her ma's people for a few years after that, till I could get back to pick her up."

"Get back?"

"I traveled 'round a mite in those days. Couldn't be bothered with a kid. Came and got her soon's she grew up enough to help me out."

"When was that?" Cale asked.

"Couple years ago. Been a lotta men sniffing after her lately, I can tell you."

It had been so long since Cale had been with a woman, just the thought of touching female flesh made his groin ache. For a moment he considered following the old man down into the valley to get a look at the girl. But he knew from experience it was worse to look and know you couldn't touch.

In the middle of winter, when he was alone, he would think about getting himself a squaw in the spring. When he was no longer snowbound, he found himself reluctant to take such a step. Once upon a time he had loved a woman, and the experience had brought him nothing but pain. Not that he had to love a woman to bed her, but neither did he underestimate the power of sexual desire. That kind of need could bring a man to his knees before a woman. Queenly presence or not — and he didn't doubt Orrin's description of his daughter — Cale Landry had vowed he would bow to no woman, ever again.

The day passed slowly. Orrin never stopped talking. Cale was glad when the sun began to set. The wind still whistled, the storm still raged, but they were snug, if not warm, in the cabin. He joined Orrin at the table while they each ate some rabbit stew. Cale left his empty bowl on the table and stood. "I'm going to get some shuteye. I've got work to do tomorrow."

"Can I talk you into a game of cards?" Orrin coaxed.

Cale was tempted. Once upon a time he had been a sharp himself. But he couldn't handle any more of Orrin's chatter, and he knew it was too much to hope the old man would hold his peace. "No," he said, then added a conciliatory, "Thanks anyway."

He left Orrin playing cards at the table while he stripped down to his long johns. He blew out two of the three lamps and snuggled under the warm furs on the bed. "Put out the light when you settle for the night," he said to Orrin.

Orrin grunted a reply.

Cale was no longer paying attention. He was thinking of a woman with long blond hair and eyes the soft blue of a robin's egg. He could feel the fullness of her lips, the smoothness of the skin at her throat. His body responded immediately to the image in his mind. His pulse pounded; his shaft hardened.

He gritted his teeth against the memories that threatened to engulf him. And reminded himself of what had come later. The lying smiles. The betrayal. The sight of her flesh joined with another man's.

Cale swallowed the grating sound of pain that sought voice. Damn Orrin Schuyler for coming into his life. For reminding him that he needed a woman. For making him want again.

He heard Orrin leave the table, and turned on his side away from the man. He didn't want that old man seeing his misery.

He hoped Orrin would blow out the lamp soon. He needed the darkness.

Cale heard footsteps and felt the old man breathing beside the bed.

"Cale? You awake?" Orrin whispered.

Cale figured if he said yes the old man would start up a conversation. He kept his breathing steady and pretended to be sound asleep.

"Good," the old man said. "This won't hurt so much."

Cale reacted an instant too late. The heavy frying pan hit the crown of his head with enough force to knock him cold.

Two

Raven woke to the sound of a man's deep, threatening voice.

"Where are my furs?"

She heard her father's strangled reply.

"Gone. Gone."

"Where's the barter you got for them?" the harsh voice demanded.

"Gambled away," her father rasped.

In the gray, predawn light she could just make out the hulking shadow crouched over her father's body. The intruder was huge and hairy, a ferocious human beast. He held a Green River skinning knife slanted across her father's throat.

She reached slowly, silently for her father's Kentucky rifle.

"Don't move!" the voice commanded.

Raven froze.

The hulking figure rose abruptly, bringing her father upright with his throat caught in one giant hand. "Who's there?" he called.

"Raven," she whispered.

"It's my daughter," Orrin said with the little air the mountain man's fierce hold allowed down his throat. "She's yours, if you'll just let me go."

Raven gasped as she realized the enormity of her father's offer.

The beast also hissed in a breath of air.

"No, Father," Raven said, struggling out from beneath the blankets she had been wrapped in and rising to her feet. There must be some other way to pay the menacing man for the furs her father had lost. She knew better than to plead with the beast. There was no mercy in the dark, haunted eyes that stared into hers.

Suddenly, her father was free. He coughed and spat, clearing his throat. "Figured you'd come hunting me," Orrin croaked, rubbing his throat. "Didn't think it would take this long, though."

The beast turned his shaggy head toward her father. "You damn near killed me!" he snarled. "Saw double for two weeks. And that was a low thing to do, hiding my clothes. I had buckskins half made when I found the set you hid under the bed."

Orrin grinned, exposing tobacco-stained teeth. "Worked though, didn't it?" He reached out to touch the sleeve of Cale's bearskin coat. "I surely hated to leave this behind, but I've got my scruples. Knew you'd need a coat."

The beast growled. "Lucky for you my horse was still there."

Orrin looked affronted. "I ain't no horse thief!"

Stealing a man's horse often condemned him to death, considering the long distances between water in the West. Thus, there was nothing lower than a horse thief, and he was killed when he was caught.

"Don't think much of a body who'd steal after accepting a man's hospitality," the beast said.

Orrin shrugged. "Couldn't help myself. Got a weakness for gambling, you know. Needed a poke and figured yours'd do."

Raven noted the look of disbelief on the beast's face.

"You lost them all?" he asked.

"Every one," Orrin confirmed. "Took near three weeks to do it, though. Too bad you didn't show up here sooner."

Raven took advantage of the opportunity to light a lantern. She stirred the fire with a stick, and when she found live coals, added kindling to build up the fire.

"How 'bout some coffee?" Orrin said. "Find yourself a seat, and we can discuss the matter of my debt to you."

Raven stiffened. So, her father had meant it when he offered her to the mountain man as though she were a pile of furs to be bartered. She kept her face turned away from the big man. She did not want to encourage his attention, and she still had hopes of escaping the trap her father had sprung on her.

The mountain man settled himself cross-legged on the ground beside her father with surprising grace. He kept his peace, listening as her father related how he had arrived early at the rendezvous site at Pierre's Hole and found a score of free trappers as well as nearly a hundred men who had hired themselves out to the Rocky Mountain and American Fur Companies. Besides the trappers, there were numerous lodges of Nez Perce and Flathead Indians.

"Found plenty who'd play cards with me, I can tell you," Orrin said. "Started out lucky. Almost doubled what I had." His slightly bucktoothed grin flashed. "Or rather, almost doubled what *you* had. Then my luck turned." He shrugged. "That's the way of it."

"That was a season's work you gambled away," the beast said. "I figured to make a couple thousand."

Orrin whistled. "That's a mighty lot, all right. But I've got something worth at least that much," he said, eyeing Raven.

"If I'd wanted a squaw, I could have bought one for a lot less than a season's worth of furs," the beast said.

Orrin's eyes narrowed. "One that speaks English? One that can cook white folk's food? One as pretty as my Raven?"

Raven felt her father's finger under her chin, forcing her face up to be observed by the mountain man. She lifted her eyes, refusing to be cowed, and met the stranger's gaze, then bit her lip to keep from gasping again.

His eyes had a hungry look. His nostrils were flared for the scent of her. His mouth, nearly hidden by a full beard, flattened to a thin line. Heavy lids hooded dark eyes in a way that did nothing to hide his naked desire. He wanted her.

Raven felt a terror she had experienced only once before, when a man had come upon her sleeping and nearly forced himself on her before she had managed to reach her knife and stab him. He had lived to embellish the tale of the Nez Perce bitch who had cut a man to pieces rather than give herself to him. Her fierce reputation had saved her from further unwanted advances at the past few rendezvous.

If her father gave her to the beast in payment of a debt, she would belong to him. She would be honor bound to obey him, to serve him in whatever he asked. And she had no doubt he would wish to couple with her. No doubt at all.

Only, she did not wish it. A surge of rebellious anger forced the words from her mouth before she could stop them. "I will work for you, as I work for my father, to repay his debt. But that is all I will do for you."

There. It was said. It was her father's problem if the beast would not accept what, and only what, she offered.

Cale couldn't take his eyes off the girl called Raven. She was beautiful beyond words, her body slim beneath the beaded buckskin dress, her face a delicate oval framed by shiny black braids from which tendrils had escaped during sleep. Her eyes were exotic, almond shaped, dark and wary. Her nose was small and straight, her mouth wide, the lips full and very, very kissable. The mixture of white and Indian blood had resulted in skin a rosy peach color that looked so soft it begged to be touched.

He wasn't the least bit pleased with the

bargain Raven had offered. She had left out the one thing he truly wanted from her! His groin tightened at the thought of bedding her. He knew deep down it was a mistake to let the old man pawn the girl off on him in payment for the furs he had stolen, especially if he agreed to the girl's terms. And yet, he couldn't bring himself to turn down the offer.

"I'll take her," he said abruptly.

"For three months," Orrin qualified. "Or thereabouts. Until the first snowfall."

Cale frowned. "Three months?"

"Or until the first snowfall," Orrin repeated. "I couldn't let her go for longer than that. I can't manage without her during the trapping season, you see."

Cale swallowed hard. Maybe Orrin was doing him a favor. If he had the girl around any longer than that, he was liable to start depending on her. Better she should go back to her father. "All right," he agreed. "Three months, or until the first snowfall."

"I will go with you," Raven said in a quiet voice, "because my father owes a debt to you. But only with the understanding that you will not take what is not offered. Otherwise, I will fight you. To the death."

Cale started to laugh at the ferocity of

her challenge. The sound died in his throat. She was serious. Her eyes flashed with defiance, and her body was tense as she waited for his response.

Raven's ultimatum certainly put a hitch in his plans for her. But Cale was quick to note that she had not said he could *never* bed her. She had said she would fight if he took *what was not offered*. Which meant that if he could win her trust, he could have her.

In days long past, Cale wouldn't have questioned his ability to convince a woman she would find pleasure in his arms. But there was something about Raven that left him wondering. He smiled wolfishly. The challenge would give him something to do to help pass the time until winter. He would have her, he decided. Somehow, some way, he would have her.

"I won't take what isn't offered," he said.

She nodded her acceptance, but the wariness didn't leave her eyes as she handed Cale a tin cup of coffee.

"You're welcome to camp here with us," Orrin offered, "and get an early start home when daylight comes."

"I need to buy supplies before I leave," Cale said.

"Sure. Take your time. Raven isn't going

anywhere. We'll be here waiting for you —"

"Raven comes with me," Cale said. "You'll understand if I don't trust you to be here when I've finished my business."

Orrin grinned. "Once burned, twice chary, eh? Raven will be ready to go when you are. Right, girl?"

Cale turned his head toward the young woman. She met his gaze without flinching.

"I will be ready."

Three

Cale glanced over his shoulder. Raven was still there. It was as though he had dreamed it all. The old man appearing on the snowy mountainside. His furs being stolen and gambled away at the rendezvous. Accepting Raven in exchange for Orrin Schuyler's debt. He hardly believed it had all happened.

Except the girl was real. He knew it from the eyes of the mountain men who followed her progress as she walked several paces behind his horse. He felt a sense of possession that was totally alien to him. He wanted to shield her from sight, so she couldn't be ogled by all those other men. Of course, he did nothing of the kind.

"Didn't figure you to take a squaw."

Cale slipped a leg over his piebald gelding and landed on both feet in front of a curly-haired man with pale blue eyes who was dressed in grease-slick buckskins. One word served as greeting and welcome. "Laidlaw."

31

Cale held out his hand, and the other man grasped it at the elbow.

"It's been a long winter, Cale," Laidlaw said. "You're a sight for sore eyes."

Cale had met Laidlaw, who was from the hills of Tennessee, his first winter in the mountains. Laidlaw had taught him everything he knew. How to survive the bitter cold, how to trap beaver, how to avoid the Blackfoot and Arikara, and how to trade with the Flathead and Nez Perce. It was Laidlaw who had encouraged him to remain a free trapper rather than hire himself out to work for one of the big fur companies. Laidlaw's advice had kept him alive and made him a rich man, though he chose to save his money, rather than spend it.

"Got time for a smoke?" Laidlaw asked.

"Sure." Cale headed with Laidlaw toward his camp.

Laidlaw's mouth curved in a crooked smile. "Aren't you forgetting something?"

Cale glanced over his shoulder and experienced a moment of chagrin. The girl. Raven had stopped in her tracks when he joined the other man. "You coming?" he called to her when she hung back.

She glanced around her at the men whose eyes ate her alive. He could almost feel the shudder that shook her small frame. "I am coming."

Cale felt that odd protectiveness again, the urge to comfort her. He shrugged it off. He knew better than to let himself feel anything for Raven Schuyler. She belonged to him, like his horse or his furs, for the period he had agreed upon with her father.

Only, there was another factor involved that made her more than that. He had been in a state of half-arousal ever since he realized she was his. He had resisted the urge to drag her into the trees and take what he wanted. Partly, it was because of the threat she had made. Partly, it was because he knew there really was no privacy to be had here. There would be time enough later, when they were alone in his cabin and certain not to be interrupted, for him to woo her into his bed.

Cale wondered whether she would really fight him. He hoped she didn't. She had to know what he wanted from her. His avid looks hadn't exactly been subtle. Still, he didn't want to hurt her. From what he had gathered, she hadn't lain with a man before. And she was tiny in comparison to his over six-foot height. She couldn't weigh more than a single pack of furs.

The mental picture of her bucking beneath him brought his shaft to hardness.

33

He grunted with annoyance at his body's fierce reaction to the mere thought of his flesh pressed close to hers. But what did he expect? He was a man who had been without a woman for better than a year. And he wanted her.

Cale welcomed Laidlaw's interruption of his carnal daydreams, until he realized the subject Laidlaw had chosen to discuss.

"Where'd you find the girl?" Laidlaw asked.

"She's payment for a debt."

Laidlaw raised a dark brow and whistled. "Must've been some debt."

"It was."

Laidlaw was an intelligent man, and he must have realized from the curtness of Cale's replies that he didn't want to discuss the woman.

"How was the trapping?" Laidlaw asked instead.

"Beaver aplenty. A few muskrat and marten."

"So you have lots of furs to trade?"

Cale's upper lip curled wryly. It seemed all roads led back to his possession of the girl. "It's a long story," he said. "I'll tell you over a cup of coffee."

Laidlaw's camp wasn't much, a ground cover thrown over a bed of pine boughs and a ring of stones where a fire had been laid. The two men settled themselves comfortably on opposite sides of the warm stones.

The valley called Pierre's Hole was about thirty miles long and fifteen wide, bounded to the west and south by low, broken ridges. The land spread north in a meadow of grass as far as the eye could see. Cale found himself with a view of three snowcapped mountain peaks called the Grand Tetons to the east.

Laidlaw set a battered speckled blue coffeepot on the fire and offered Cale some tobacco for his pipe.

Cale realized Raven was still standing nearby, holding the lead rope of a newly purchased mule loaded with his supplies for the coming year — gunpowder, a new ax, a dozen five-pound steel beaver traps with double springs, and the scented castoreum to attract the beaver, with which he baited the traps. He had also purchased foodstuffs he craved — sugar, coffee, flour, beans, and bacon.

Raven was apparently waiting for permission, or a command, to sit. He started to say "Join us" and realized that wasn't what he wanted, after all. It wasn't that he thought she would be embarrassed by the discussion of her father's perfidy, but rather that it would be uncomfortable to have her listening with that martyred expression to every word that came from his mouth.

"Gather some wood for the fire," he said.

Raven tied the mule's lead to a nearby scrub tree and turned wordlessly to obey him.

Before she had taken three steps he said, "Don't go beyond my sight."

Raven shot him a quick look of . . . disdain? — before heading across the meadow toward a stream fed by rivulets and mountain springs. It was bordered with willow and cottonwood that had grown so thick it was nearly impassable.

Cale found himself watching the gentle sashay of her hips as she moved away, which set the buckskin fringe on her skirt to swaying. When he turned back he saw Laidlaw grinning at him.

"She's prime, all right," Laidlaw said.

Cale was grateful for the beard that hid his flush. "She's payment for a debt."

"You already said that," Laidlaw replied with a chuckle.

Cale shook his head like a baited bear. "It's not like I planned to get myself a woman," he began. "It just happened."

Laidlaw poured Cale a cup of coffee and handed it to him. "I'm envious," he admitted. "Have you had her yet?"

"We just settled the debt this morning."

"She's the one who stabbed Jack Pelter a few years back, isn't she?"

"I wouldn't know."

"She is," Laidlaw confirmed. "Man had so many cuts on him by the time she was through, they started calling him Ribbon Jack." He pursed his lips. "Naw. You haven't had her yet."

"What makes you say that?"

Laidlaw smirked. "Don't see any marks on you."

"What happens between me and the girl is none of your business," Cale snapped.

"Ain't that a sack o' hell. Man's got a pretty woman for his bed and won't share the details with his best friend."

"Get your own woman. There's plenty to be had here."

"Not like that one," Laidlaw said wistfully.

Cale didn't dispute him. He himself thought that Raven was an extraordinary woman. She carried herself with a sense of presence that was every bit as majestic as her father had suggested. Cale was surprised to hear she was the one who had cut up Ribbon Jack. He had seen the slashes on the man's face at the Wind River rendezvous two years ago. He would have to make sure Raven didn't have a knife on her when he was ready to bed her. But then, he planned to have her naked. There would be no place for her to hide a knife.

"You gonna tell me what happened to those furs of yours?" Laidlaw said.

Cale explained everything that had happened over the past month, from finding Orrin Schuyler in the mountains, to their confrontation that morning.

Laidlaw whistled in appreciation. "Sounds like you're lucky you came through with a whole skin — no pun intended."

Cale grinned. His smile faded as he caught sight of Raven returning with a load of firewood. Not far from the stream, she was surrounded by a rowdy group of drunken men.

Without bothering to excuse himself, he rose, grabbed his Hawken rifle, and headed toward her.

Raven had spent the better part of the morning trying to reconcile herself to her fate. The more she thought about the situation, the less she liked it. The man-beast was much larger than she was. Even if she remained constantly on guard, there was always the chance he might catch her unawares and take what he wanted by force.

Despite his shaggy-haired, beastlike appearance, Cale Landry did not appear to be a brutal man, but appearances could be deceiving. Her uncle had seemed a kindly man. She had been more than willing to stay with him when her father had brought her to live with the Nez Perce after her mother had died. But Two Bears had been a bully and a brute. She had suffered many a bruise before she learned to stay out of his way.

Raven had been ready and willing to leave the Nez Perce camp when her father returned for her several years later. Though Orrin Schuyler worked her like a beast of burden, at least he did not slap or cuff her. As they spent more time together, they had struck a wordless bargain in which she helped him with the work that must be done, and he kept her safe from the men who sought to use her for their pleasure.

Only, in the end, her father had sacrificed her to save himself. She had only agreed to the bargain because . . . because

39

she had seen something in Cale Landry's face beyond mere lust for a woman. His eyes had held a longing, a loneliness she had recognized and understood, because it dwelled within her as well.

Raven forced her thoughts away from contemplation of a physical joining between her and the huge, hairy beast. She could not help feeling afraid. She reassured herself with the knowledge that she had told Cale — it felt strange to give the beast a name — that she would not lie with him. If he tried to force her, he would find out she meant what she had said.

Raven became aware of a group of men coming toward her at about the same time she realized she didn't have her knife. It was a fatal error to be without a weapon, a mistake she had not made for a long time. But the events of the morning had been extraordinary, and she had been concerned about getting away from Cale and having time alone to think, so she had left her knife with her pack on the mule.

Slowly, carefully, Raven shifted the bundle of sticks off her shoulders and down to the tall grass at her feet. To her dismay, the drunken men didn't stay in a group. They shifted around her, like a pack of wolves stalking its quarry, making it impossible to keep her eyes on all of them at the same time.

One shouted to draw her attention, while another rushed her from behind. Raven eluded him and darted between two others, who both grabbed for her and ended up running into each other. She sprinted for the spot where she had left Cale, but she hadn't gotten far before she was dragged down from behind. She lashed out with her feet, catching one of her tormentors in the shin with a lucky blow. Another man took his place.

The thunder of a Hawken was followed by the painful yelp of one of the men who held her down. He fell sideways with an awful howl. The rest of the men froze in a tableau of stunned surprise that made Raven want to laugh. She was too busy yanking her dress down over her exposed thighs to find humor in the situation.

"The woman is mine," a harsh voice announced. "Anybody wants to dispute that can deal with me."

To Raven's astonishment, the men each took a cautious step backward. It seemed no one wanted to contest Cale's claim on her. One look at his face and she could see why. Death waited for the unlucky soul who challenged him.

Raven stumbled to her feet in time to see that there was one foolhardy man who seemed determined to fight. Undaunted, he stood with fists perched on hips and feet spread wide.

It was Ribbon Jack.

Raven felt a shiver of revulsion travel her spine. On his best day, Ribbon Jack had not been an attractive man. Now, with several bright pink scars across his right cheek, he looked even less agreeable. His brown eyes glittered with malice as he eyed her. She made an unconscious move backward toward Cale.

He put a hand on her shoulder and shoved her behind him, handing her his Hawken. "Stay out of the way," he ordered.

Cale took his eyes off Ribbon Jack just long enough to make sure that Raven was free of harm's way. It was a mistake that nearly cost him his life.

Ribbon Jack lunged with a knife he had pulled from the sheath tied between his shoulders. His blow would have caught Cale in the heart if he hadn't thrown up his arm at the last instant. Instead, the knife caught in the thick sleeve of his bearskin coat.

In seconds the two men were surrounded by the drunken crowd, which was ready to enjoy this entertainment as a welcome substitute for the fun they had been denied with the squaw.

Cale hadn't realized how much he needed this fight. It gave him the opportunity to release the anger he felt over being fooled by Orrin Schuyler. It helped that Ribbon Jack was a strong adversary. Cale was taller than the other man, but Ribbon Jack was thick with muscle. Apparently Jack hadn't drunk much of the rotgut that passed for alcohol among the mountain men. His reflexes were quick, and Cale was hard-set to keep from being stabbed, even though he now had a knife in his hand as well.

Now that he was locked in mortal combat, Cale realized he didn't want to kill the other man. Not that he hadn't killed before, and wouldn't again, but it seemed to him that Ribbon Jack had already suffered for his encounter with Raven. Living with the knowledge that he had been bested by a squaw was punishment enough for any man.

Cale feinted in one direction, but held his place. When Ribbon Jack lunged, Cale managed to catch the man's wrist and forced the knife from Jack's hand. Jack would have continued the fight with his fists, but Cale held the tip of his Green River knife to the other man's throat and said, "I'm satisfied. Enough for you?"

Ribbon Jack had no choice but to grunt his assent. Once he was free, he snatched his knife from the ground and returned it to the sheath between his shoulders. "That woman is trouble," he muttered to Cale. "She should be taken care of."

Cale was left with no doubt how Ribbon Jack would "take care of" Raven if he ever got his hands on her. But he said, "I'll take care of her. You just make sure you keep your distance."

Ribbon Jack didn't bother to answer him, just turned and headed away by himself, too humiliated to try and join the men who had watched the fight. They never missed him. They were already passing around the kettle of rotgut.

Cale headed back to the campfire, where he found Laidlaw waiting for him.

"Business finished?" Laidlaw asked.

"I can't help feeling sorry for the man," Cale said. He shoved a hand through his long black hair as he settled down beside Laidlaw. He found his Hawken lying beside the fire, but no sign of Raven. "Where's the girl?"

Laidlaw shrugged. "Took her pack off your mule and headed toward the trees. Figured you must have told her to go hide herself somewheres so she couldn't get into any more trouble."

Cale swore a blue streak. He came to his feet like an avenging fury, Hawken in hand. "Damn that squaw! I knew it was a mistake to get myself involved with a woman."

"What's wrong?" Laidlaw asked.

"I didn't send her anywhere," Cale said. "Damned female must've run off."

Laidlaw laughed. "Why not just let her go?"

"She belongs to me," Cale said in a hard voice. "Until the first snow falls, she's mine. And I don't give up what's mine."

He didn't bother explaining his fierce desire to possess the woman. He didn't quite understand it himself. He only knew he wasn't going to let her go.

Cale mounted his horse, grabbed the lead rope on the mule, and headed in the direction Raven had gone. She wouldn't get far on foot. And when he caught up to her . . . she would pay.

Four

Raven was woken by a hand clamped over her mouth. She struggled to rise, but a heavy weight bore her down. It was pitch black, and there was nothing to tell her who her captor was. Only she knew. From the musky smell of him. From the size of him. From the harsh sound of his voice when he spoke.

"Don't scream," Cale said.

The thought had never crossed her mind. She felt a breathless, paralyzing terror. She had run away, and he had come after her. And caught her. He was likely furious. Men, she had discovered, did not like to have their will thwarted by women. And this man was a stranger to her. She had no idea what form his revenge would take.

The hand that covered her mouth also half-covered her nose, so she had difficulty breathing. She grabbed for Cale's wrist and shoved with all her might to move it enough so she could catch her breath.

"Don't bother struggling. You can't get free," he said.

Her fear made it even more difficult to draw breath, so she fought him harder, clawing at his large, powerful hand with her nails. Her efforts were futile.

Then she thought of the knife she had tied to her thigh before she began her flight, where it would be readily available in just such an emergency. She abruptly stopped fighting and reached surreptitiously toward the slit in her skirt that allowed her access to the weapon.

"That's better," Cale said.

She noticed his voice almost crooned, as though he were attempting to calm a wild animal caught in the steel jaws of a trap. He did not know it yet, but she was fully capable of being as vicious as a cornered wildcat. The moment she was armed with the claw-sharp knife now resting in its sheath, he would see he had underestimated her.

Raven drew the knife and plunged it toward Cale's heart all in one swift movement, because she knew she wouldn't get a second chance. Cale was bigger and stronger. Her only advantage was the element of surprise.

She heard his grunted "Oooff" and felt

the knife catch on something. Suddenly his hand fell away from her mouth.

"Beast!" she hissed. "Animal! I hope I've killed you!"

She felt the warm wetness of blood on her hand and struggled frantically to free herself from beneath him. His legs straddled her waist, and as he fell forward with his full weight, she was trapped beneath him.

"No!" Raven shoved against Cale's shoulders in an attempt to move him, but without success. She bucked with her hips beneath what she believed to be his dying body, hoping to move him off of her.

To her dismay she felt him shift his hips farther into the cradle of her thighs. It became immediately, undeniably plain that he was not a dead man. For in that most intimate of places she could feel the length of him, hot and hard and ready for a stabbing wound that she was convinced would be the death of her.

"No. Please," she whispered. "I . . ." She had to swallow over the painful lump of fear in her throat before she could continue. "I will not run away again. I will serve you as I promised. If only you will not . . . will not touch me."

She held herself stiff beneath him, unyielding, ready to fight, drawing all her resources together for the battle she feared was about to begin.

To her relief and astonishment, he grunted once and rolled off her onto his back.

She clambered to her feet and stumbled backward several steps to put some distance between them. Raven wasn't sure why Cale hadn't taken her, since he obviously wasn't wounded badly enough to affect his ability to do the deed, but she wasn't going to give him a chance to change his mind. The night air was frigid without the striped wool blanket she had wrapped herself in. She felt, rather than saw, the clouds that formed as she panted, drawing explosive breaths into starving lungs.

"This wound needs some attention," Cale said. "Build up the fire so you can see what you're doing."

Raven hesitated only a moment before she dropped to her knees and felt for the stones she had laid in a circle to keep the fire from spreading. She stirred the ashes and found a glowing ember to which she added some dry grass and a few twigs until it burst into flame. In that tiny, orange light she saw Cale Landry's face for the first time since she had left him fighting Ribbon Jack.

His eyes gleamed in the dark, like some beast of prey. His teeth were bared in a grimace of pain. His fingers, shiny with blood, framed the hilt of her knife. It was clear that the bearskin coat had taken the brunt of her thrust. Only the mere tip of the knife was imbedded in his skin. She was disgusted to see that she had only caught his shoulder, missing his heart by several inches.

"Go ahead and pull it out," Cale said. "I'd do it myself, but it's at an awkward angle for me to reach."

Raven's lips flattened in distaste. The sight of blood made her sick. She had learned, out of necessity, to swallow her gorge and to work with her head averted from whatever animal she was slaughtering for supper. But she would need to pay attention to what she was doing in order to pull the knife from Cale's shoulder without doing him further injury. Not that she would have minded if he suffered further, but she feared that if she provoked him by hurting him, he would finish what he had started.

The big man made no sound as the knife came free in her hand. She stared at the tip darkened with blood, both fascinated and nauseated. She had started to sway dizzily when he plucked the knife from her fingers and put it down out of sight.

"There's water in my canteen to clean up this blood. Have you got anything you can use as a bandage?"

He was sitting up now, slipping the bear-skin coat off his arms so it created a puddle of fur around his hips. Raven had never seen Cale without the coat, and she was surprised to discover that it wasn't the fur that had made him look so big. He *was* big, with shoulders as broad as an ancient tree. It was equally apparent there wasn't a shred of fat on him. His body narrowed to a slim waist and his legs were long and muscular.

She approached him with the canteen she had taken from where it hung on his saddle. "Perhaps, since your shirt is already covered with blood, we could use it to wash your wound."

Cale looked at the long john shirt that was soaked with blood at the shoulder. He made a disgruntled sound and started to draw the shirt up over his head. He hissed in a breath of air as he jarred the knife wound. He handed the shirt to Raven.

Raven forced her eyes away from the

sight that now greeted her. The mountain man was an awesome being, half-naked as he was. The promise of strength she had seen when he dropped the coat was fulfilled in the man sitting before her. It surprised her to discover that, although he had a patch of dark hair in the center of his chest, he was not the hairy beast she had suspected. A thin line of black down ran into his buckskin trousers. She resisted an urge to see if it was as soft as it looked.

Raven lifted her gaze guiltily and found herself staring into lazy, hooded black eyes that seemed to laugh at her.

"See anything you like?" he asked.

Raven was grateful for the dark that hid her flush of embarrassment. "Lean back," she said curtly, "and I will clean your wound."

Cale obeyed, and Raven dabbed at the wound with the dampened long john shirt until most of the blood was cleared away. She kept swallowing her gorge, hoping she wouldn't humiliate herself by losing the contents of her stomach before she had finished.

"It needs to be stitched," she said when she could see the extent of the wound.

Cale pursed his lips. "There's a needle and thread in my pack."

Raven used the excuse he gave her to get away. Once her back was turned to Cale, she took several deep breaths to clear the stench of blood from her nostrils. It was the smell, the coppery, oily odor of blood that was the worst. Sometimes, she would tie a bandanna around her face to avoid it. But, she wasn't willing to display her weakness to this man, at least not so soon in their relationship. She would have to use the other remedy she had found that sometimes worked. She would put herself in another place, doing something else, and not think about the blood.

She remembered a time when her mother had taken her to the river to swim. The water was icy cold, and they had laughed as the trout nibbled at their toes. The sun had sparkled on the water, and the wind had soughed through the firs in a haunting cascade. It was a nearly perfect day, a happy day. Now, the only image of her mother that remained was a look of tenderness in a pair of dark eyes and a sweet, gentle smile.

Raven focused on that memory as she opened Cale's packs, searching for the needle and thread. With Cale directing her where to look, she found what she needed. Raven took her time threading the precious steel needle, then settled on her knees at Cale's side, where she would have access to the wound. She took a deep breath and thought of sparkling water and the heady scent of pines.

"This will hurt," she warned him.

"It won't be the first time I've been stitched," he said. "Do what you have to do."

It was only after he mentioned it that she realized there were more than a few scars on his upper body. She had been so overwhelmed by the whole of him, she hadn't looked at the parts. She noticed a round, smooth scar near his collarbone that appeared to be from a bullet. There were three stripes that she realized had been left by the claws of some wild animal. She reached out tentatively to touch them and felt Cale flinch.

Raven glanced up and was caught by the look in his eyes. His gaze seemed soft, almost tender. She quickly lowered her eyes to the unusual scar, but not before she felt a peculiar warmth flood her body.

"Cougar?" she asked as she softly traced the marks.

"Grizzly," he replied.

His voice was husky, and the sound lifted the hairs on her neck. "Big brute I've come to call Three Toes, seeing as how he lost the rest to a trap I laid for him." Cale touched the striped scar with his own fingertips. "He repaid me for the insult. We've had a war going ever since."

Raven couldn't help respecting a man who was willing to face down a grizzly. She shuddered at the thought of confronting one of the huge animals. Her only previous encounter with a grizzly had resulted in the loss of a childhood friend who was mauled to death. She had developed a deathly fear of bears.

"You going to stitch me up, or sit there thinking about it some more?"

Raven felt a flash of resentment. He was lucky she was willing to help him. But she had learned from past experience to hide the temper that sometimes flared and got her into trouble. Instead she said, "I don't want to hurt you." She added in a taunting voice, "Do you want to drink some whiskey before I begin?" She would soon see just how brave he was.

"No," he said. "Just get it done."

Raven took a deep breath and let it out. She swallowed hard, then stuck the needle into his flesh.

He didn't make a sound.

She looked into his eyes and saw the

pain he hadn't expressed. She worked quickly, pulling the flesh together with tiny stitches, careful not to pucker the skin, keeping it flat so it would heal cleanly.

"This is the last stitch," she said.

"Damn good thing," he muttered.

As she tied the last knot, she realized there were beads of sweat on his forehead. His hands were clenched into fists. She had thought he must not feel pain quite as other men did, but now she saw he had only endured it well. She could not help admiring him for it. It was the Indian way, to act stoically in the face of suffering. She compared her father's howls to Cale's silence and found herself wondering in what other ways he might be different from other men.

Cale shivered, and she realized he must be cold. The air was frigid, and he was naked to the waist. Without saying a word, she threaded the needle through the shoulder of her buckskin dress so she wouldn't lose it, then stood and reached for the bearskin coat to draw around him.

"Thanks," he said.

"Are you hungry?" Raven had asked because she knew from experience that a man with an empty stomach was more troublesome than one who had eaten. If she were to tame the beast, she had best keep him fed.

"I need sleep more than food. Let's get some shut-eye. I want to get an early start in the morning."

Raven felt Cale's eyes on her as she cleaned the needle and returned it to his pack. She rinsed the blood from his long john shirt as best she could, then laid it on a bush to dry. Finally, there was nothing else to do. Unfortunately, he was sitting on her blanket. When she started to pull it out from under him, he stopped her.

"Uh-uh. You'll be sleeping here, where I can keep an eye on you."

"I will not run," she said in a breathless voice.

He snickered. "You've been too much in your father's company for me to trust you. Come here, Raven. I want you beside me."

"You promised —"

"I'm not going to touch a hair on your head," Cale said irritably. "Just get your tail over here so I can get some sleep." He lifted an edge of her blanket, making it plain that he expected her to roll up in it and sleep within his arms.

Raven debated the wisdom of running again. He would be weaker with the wound she had given him. The look in his eyes convinced her he would never let her go. And the next time he caught her, he might not be so willing to forego the pleasures of the flesh.

She lowered herself onto the blanket with her back to him and felt him circle her with both the wool and a bearskin-clad arm. He pulled her snug against him, so her bottom spooned into his groin. She tried shifting away from him, but to no avail.

"Lie still," he said. "It'll be warmer if we sleep this way."

She couldn't deny that. In fact, a fierce heat had suffused her body. Her heart thumped a brisk tattoo and her whole body was wired taut with a strange tension.

"Raven," he whispered against her ear. "You're about the most beautiful thing I've ever seen in the mountains. And that's saying a lot."

Frightened by the sensual tone of his voice, by the delicious tickle his mouth created, she shook her head as though a fly had buzzed her ear, catching him in the nose.

He grabbed one of her braids and wrapped it around his fist. "Be still," he murmured. "Be still."

His other hand flattened against her stomach, pressing her back into his groin. He was aroused. She could feel the length and hardness of him. Her breath came in shallow pants. Her heart thundered in her breast.

Raven was aware of each fingertip splayed across her belly. Of the warmth of his breath in her ear. She felt dizzy, almost as if she were going to faint. She resented Cale touching her but was forced to admit he wasn't hurting her. She was ready to fight him, tooth and claw, if he tried to do what it was clear he was primed and ready to do.

Only, to her dismay — disgust, displeasure, delight — the next thing she heard from Cale Landry was a long, stertorous snore.

Five

"This is it." Cale watched Raven closely to see her reaction to his cabin. It wasn't much, but it was home. He tried to see it with a woman's eyes, but it was all too familiar to him. He admired the table hand hewn from Douglas fir and the two chairs on either side of it. It was odd, he realized, that a man who lived alone would have *two* chairs. Had he unconsciously longed for company?

Well, there was only *one* bed. He hadn't wanted a woman. But he had one. Or rather, there was one in his cabin. He didn't think he was going to be having her anytime soon.

"What do you think?" Cale could have bitten his tongue as soon as he said the words. What did he care what she thought? She was just a squaw come to spend a little time here. It was irrelevant whether his cabin met her approval. She would be staying here whether it did, or not.

She still hadn't said anything, and he

found himself feeling anxious. Hadn't he come up here to live all alone just so he wouldn't have to worry about some woman judging the way he lived his life? So he wouldn't have to bend over backwards to please a woman who would betray him in the end, anyway?

"Well?" he demanded. His voice was harsh with the disgust he felt that her opinion mattered, and he was angry with her for intruding on the privacy he had jealously protected for the past ten years. "What do you think?"

"It's filthy," Raven said. "And it stinks."

Cale was stung by her condemnation. "You'll just have to get used to it," he snarled.

"No," she said, shaking her head. "I will not live like this. Even a bear does not sleep in a foul den."

"Is this some sort of excuse for you to break our bargain?" he demanded.

She looked right at him, and he was frozen by the scorn in her dark eyes. "I will abide by the bargain my father made. But I will not sleep in a hovel." She headed for the door.

He grabbed her arm as she passed him and pulled her close so they were nose to nose. "It's going to get mighty cold outside come dark," he said.

"I do not plan to sleep outside," she retorted.

"You just said —"

"I will clean this place and make it fit for human beings."

As he started to release his grip she added in a soft voice, "You have lived alone too long, my beast."

"What did you call me?"

He saw the flush rise under her peach skin to stain her high, wide cheekbones. Her eyes flashed, first with fear, then with defiance.

"Beast. I called you beast."

He dropped her arm as though she had scalded him. He hadn't thought a woman could wound him again. Especially not one he wasn't in love with. One he wouldn't give a pound of coffee for, let alone a pack of furs.

Only he hadn't given a single pound of coffee. Or a single pack of furs, for that matter. He had given an entire season's catch, nearly two thousand dollars worth of skins, for the privilege of being insulted by this woman in his own home.

Cale found himself helpless to strike her. He wasn't in the habit of brutalizing women and children. But he was angry enough to do it. Which was strange in itself. How had she gotten under his skin so quickly? He felt humiliated by her accusation that he lived like an animal. He wasn't an animal. He was a man. Maybe his habits had become a little slovenly, but there had been no one to please but himself. And he hadn't been a harsh taskmaster.

He looked again at his cabin. Instead of feeling pride for the strong, hand-hewn table and huge pine bed he had made with his own hands, instead of remembering the satisfaction he had felt the first time he lit the black, potbellied stove he had taken the trouble to cart all the way up into the mountains, he felt shame.

Dozens of beaver traps lay in piles on the floor. Willow frames for stretching fur hung haphazardly on pegs. The pot on the stove was half-filled with the stew he hadn't finished before he had left the cabin. That must be responsible for at least some of the stench she smelled. The bedcover he had stitched around grass ticking was stained with mud, but he remembered having put his dirty moccasins on it a time or two. Of course, there was a layer of dust over everything. He often worked with the door open, and he considered dust a fact of life.

Even though he was willing to concede the place was a mess, he didn't like feeling guilty for it. For a second he considered forbidding her to touch anything. But that would have been cutting off his nose to spite his face. After all, if she wasn't going to let him take what he wanted from her, he might as well get some good out of her over the next few months. If she wanted to play maid of all work, that was fine with him.

"If you don't like what you see, you can clean it up."

"Will you help me?"

"Hell, no! I won't!" Cale was surprised at the force of his response. He couldn't remember the last time he had shouted. He felt a little ridiculous when he realized who he was shouting at and how she had provoked him into it.

"You want it clean, you clean it," he said emphatically.

"Where is your broom?" she asked.

"I —" He didn't have a broom. Hadn't seen the need for one. Until now. "I'll make one for you," he said between clenched teeth.

She nodded in that smug, superior, self-satisfied way a woman had of looking at a man when she had made her point.

"All right, so I live like a pig. Welcome to the sty!" With those words he marched out the door, unable to face the pitying, sympathetic look she plastered on her face, as though he were some poor, feebleminded simpleton who didn't know any better. Well, he wasn't quite simple yet. He was smart enough to get the hell out of here before she made him feel like an insect, instead of just an animal.

Raven watched Cale's flight from the cabin with ill-concealed triumph. He had abandoned the field of battle and left her the victor. When she looked around at the hovel she had won, she felt more despair than hope. She hadn't exaggerated when she told Cale his cabin was little better than some animal's burrow. She feared she would never get the stink out of it.

Raven had taken only one deep breath, and it had been enough to force her to resort to shallow panting. The cabin reeked. The smell of muskrat caught her in the nose, making her wrinkle it to trap the smell, and then flatten it to force it out. But the stench of beaver was worse. The smell caught in the back of her throat, making it impossible to swallow.

Raven noticed Cale had left the door

open when he stomped out. She crossed to the threshold and stood there breathing deep. Here the fresh scent of pine exhilarated her. Perhaps she had been wrong wishing for a permanent home all those years she had been a wanderer. Indians moved their camps away from the offal that collected over time. Orrin had moved because he was always one step ahead of whoever he had most recently flim-flammed.

She had come across a cabin one bitterly cold winter as a child and imagined what it would be like, snug and warm inside. It had been a fantasy of hers for years, to live in such a home. Now she was condemned — that was the only word she could think of that fit the awful circumstances — to live here until the first snowfall.

She looked around her. The dirt could be cleaned away, the clutter could be put away, but the smell? She eyed the skin that covered the window. Perhaps if she removed it a breeze would blow through and take the worst of the stench with it. She headed for the window without thinking about what Cale would say when he discovered what she had done.

"What the hell do you think you're doing?"

Raven froze with the parchment skin rolled and tucked under her arm. Cale loomed in the doorway with a makeshift broom in his hands.

"I guess I don't really need to ask what you're doing," he continued when she didn't answer him. "I can see for myself. What I have to ask is, why?"

Cale felt foolish standing there with a broom in his hand, and he felt a rising rage at her violation of his home. "I figured you'd want to sweep the place out, not take it apart," he said with an ironic twist of his lips.

"I only wanted to get some more fresh air inside." She gave a little shrug. "Taking the skin from the window seemed the fastest, easiest way to accomplish that. I promise to put it back again."

She held the skin out to him, as though he would know what to do with it. She gave him a teasing smile and said, "It won't bite."

He felt a shimmer of something dangerously like desire traverse his spine. That smile of hers was lethal. It gave a man ideas that could get him into serious trouble. Cale wasn't someone who took chances. He traded her the broom for the skin and stalked outside, away from the threat she posed. Once he was back in the sunshine he stared at the skin as though it might, indeed, bite him. And wondered what he was supposed to do with it. He set it down near the door.

"Hellfire and damnation," he muttered. He unpacked the mule, then took his horse to the shed to brush it down. When he was done, he stepped out of the lean-to and stared at his cabin. The door hung wide open. She had been here only an hour and already she had taken it over. He was afraid to cross his own threshold because *she* was in there. Well, he'd be damned before he'd let her toss him out like so much garbage.

Cale stomped back inside his cabin, stood there for a moment staring at the bare floors, then headed for the potbellied stove to heat himself a cup of coffee. Which was when he saw the coffeepot was missing.

He refused to ask her where it was. It had to be here somewhere. He walked over and stood beside the stove and looked around. He couldn't find it anywhere.

Which was when he noticed the raggedy sleeve of some old long johns protruding from the stove lid. *She was burning his clothes!* He wasn't about to call her on it, knowing she would be bound to point out the obviously worn out condition of the garment.

"Can I get you something?" she asked.

"I want a cup of coffee," he said. "I can make it myself, if you'll tell me what you did with the coffeepot."

"I left it down at the creek, with the other dirty dishes, to soak. I will go get it now. You sit down and be comfortable while I am gone."

She stood the broom up against the wall and started out the door.

That was when the guilt hit him. He couldn't very well sit there doing nothing while she traipsed down to Wolf Creek all by her lonesome. Anything might happen to her. Old Three Toes was out there, not to mention savages, and who knew what-all. "I'll go with you," he said, hurrying for the door.

"There is no need for both of us to go," she said. "I will stay here and keep on working. You will find everything straight down the hill from the front door. The dishes ought to be well soaked enough now to scrub out easily with a little sand."

Cale wasn't sure how he had been bamboozled. He only knew he had. Here he was on his way down to the creek *to wash*

69

dishes. And he didn't even have the woman for company! He couldn't remember the last time he had actually washed his dishes. He sort of wiped them clean with his fingers, or waited for the food to dry and scraped it out. One year? Two? Probably more than that, he realized. Maybe she was right. Maybe he really was an animal.

It was a disturbing thought, and one which Cale chose not to contemplate as he washed the dishes. Considering how long it had been since they had seen sand and water, they came clean surprisingly easily. He wondered when he had stopped observing the rules of a more civilized society.

Cleanliness was an easy one to let go, because it was a sin of omission. One merely had to *not* do something. Like wash dishes. Or bathe. It dawned on him suddenly, that if she had found the house odoriferous, she might have made the same judgment about *him!*

Before he could stop himself, he pulled off his moccasins. Then he yanked off the long john shirt — it was the same blood-stained one she had only rinsed out after stabbing him — then shimmied out of his buckskins and long john drawers. He waded into Wolf Creek, remembering immediately why he had given up bathing.

The water was frigid. It was fed from a mountain spring and stayed cold all year round. He splashed himself a couple of times but realized as he looked down at his skin, that it was as dirty as his dishes had been, caked with grime that had layered over years of neglect.

Cale hissed as he lowered himself until he was sitting in the stream. The water barely came to his waist here, and it rushed by, leaving goose bumps the size of hen's eggs on his arms. The bottom of the stream was more rocks than sand, but by moving a few out of the way he came up with a handful of pebbly sand that he used to scrub briskly at his skin. He was careful to wash around his stitches, but he rinsed them clean with the cold, clear water.

He rubbed until the flesh on his arms was raw, and finally saw, beneath the grit, his own pale skin. He would have been hard pressed to identify his feelings at the moment. Disbelief was foremost. How could he have gone so long without a bath? How had an Indian woman shamed him into taking one? And if, as he had told himself over the years, bathing wasn't important, why did it feel so good to be clean again?

★ ★ ★

Raven hadn't intended to maneuver Cale
into washing dishes, and when she thought
about it as she swept the cabin, she began
to regret the impish impulse that had provoked her into sending him down to the
creek. It was an indisputable fact that
washing dishes was woman's work. Maybe
that partly explained the filth. She knew a
man could lose face with other men if he
was caught doing a job that was meant
only for women. Cale had been without a
woman for years; thus, the woman's work
had remained undone.

Raven snorted in disgust. She couldn't
imagine a *woman* living in such filth because a *man* wasn't around to help with the
work! She had never understood men, and
she supposed she never would. It had surprised her when Cale hadn't argued about
washing the dishes. But he had been gone
a long time and still hadn't returned. Perhaps she should go and find out what was
keeping him.

She stopped outside the small, one room
cabin and turned to admire the construc-
tion. That, at least, had been done with
care. The logs were fitted snugly at the
corners and were chinked with mud and
grass to keep out the cold winter winds. Of

course, she mused with a smile, the same windproofing that kept the cabin warm in winter was what had kept in the rancid smells that permeated the place.

She was still smiling when she reached the creek. The smile slowly faded as she realized the odd stone in the creek bed wasn't a stone at all. It was moving. It had arms and legs and a furry beard. Cale Landry was sitting buck naked in the middle of the water. He was taking a bath!

Beside the creek, stacked haphazardly, were the dishes she had sent him to fetch. They were clean, she quickly noted. As he soon would be, as well.

Her smile returned, and with it a bubble of laughter.

Cale was appalled to discover Raven standing on the bank gawking at him. More to the point, he was astonished that anyone had been able to sneak up on him like that. Over the years he had honed his senses to detect even the slightest noise. Staying alive depended on staying alert. So how the hell had he ended up getting caught with his pants down like some Eastern yokel?

"Shall I come in and wash your back?" she teased.

Cale had a vivid image of what it would

be like to have her standing behind him, equally naked, scrubbing his back. Despite the cold water, his pulse leaped. "Come on in," he said.

The smile froze on her face. "The water's cold."

"I ought to know," he replied. "I'm sitting in it. Come on in," he urged. "My back could use a scrubbing."

He hadn't expected her to comply. After all, she hadn't done much else he had asked of her. To his amazement, she slipped off her moccasins and waded into the water. The fringe of her dress floated on top, acting like lures for the fish, as she walked toward him.

She traversed a wide berth around him, so she ended up behind him. He tensed, waiting for the first touch of her fingertips against his skin. The water didn't feel cold any more. On the contrary, he had lit his very own bonfire. Cale was chagrined at how swiftly and powerfully his body responded to her presence. He brought his knees up to hide his arousal. He didn't figure it was any of her business.

Raven told herself that the only reason she had succumbed to Cale's taunt to wash his back was because she would be the one to benefit. After all, so long as she was cleaning the house, she might as well go all the way and clean the man who lived in it.

As she stood there, staring at his broad, muscular back, she felt an urge to caress the smooth skin that covered bone and sinew. Instead, she reached down and scooped up a handful of coarse sand, applying it to his back and rubbing energetically.

"Ouch! You're going to take off a layer of skin," Cale protested.

"And four layers of dirt," she retorted. "When was the last time you took a bath?"

He didn't answer. He wouldn't lie, and he wasn't about to tell the truth. Instead, he sat there in mute defiance, daring her to rub him raw.

She damn near did.

Once she was started, Raven took her work to heart. She used all her strength, rubbing until Cale's skin was pink all over, a sign that it was finally clean.

Then she scooped handfuls of the frigid water and rinsed off the sand, painfully aware that the water had to be stinging his raw skin.

He never made a sound.

She suddenly felt remorse for her harsh treatment. Surely Cale didn't deserve her anger. It was her father who had put her in this position. The mountain man had not been given much choice. It was either take her or forfeit any payment at all for his skins. Of course, he could simply have killed her father. All things considered, he had chosen the more humane alternative.

So why had she scrubbed his skin raw? More to the point, why had he allowed it?

Raven was confused by her conflicting feelings about the mountain man. She should have been terrified to be alone with him, naked as he was. Instead, she had been drawn to touch him more. She had been rough because she was daring Cale to respond with roughness. That would have given her the excuse she needed to put him in the same category as Ribbon Jack.

But Cale had endured her ministrations without so much as a grunt of discomfort. In so doing, he had planted a small seed of trust, the suggestion that with this man she did not need to fear his strength. His calm acceptance of her hands on him led her to indulge her curiosity about how it would feel to touch what she found so attractive to the eye.

Raven ran her fingertips soothingly over Cale's pinkened shoulders. Down across the muscular back. Then back up the narrow indentation along his spine. His skin was warm and resilient. The muscles flexed involuntarily beneath her fingertips, and she could feel his massive strength.

Cale tried not to move, because he didn't want her to stop what she was doing. She was caressing him, touching him in ways that made his body sing hosanna. As much as he wanted to return the favor, he felt certain that if she realized what she was doing, she would stop. So he held himself still, as though he had come upon a fawn in the forest, and didn't want to spook it into running.

Her fingertips slid up to his nape, and his neckhairs stood on end. A frisson of desire skittered down his spine. He couldn't stand it. He would surely die if he couldn't touch her soon.

"Dammit to hell!" He rose in a flurry of spraying water and turned to grab her in his arms.

It was then he realized why she had stopped. She was staring with a look of horror at the opposite bank.

It was occupied by Old Three Toes.

Six

Raven's glance had snagged on the immense grizzly that stood on its hind legs, sharp-toothed jaws agape, a malevolent presence. They were trapped without weapons, virtually helpless, in the center of Wolf Creek. She would have screamed, except she was too frightened to draw breath.

Cale's leap from the water had startled the beast, which turned and fled.

Unfortunately, it didn't go far.

"We're trapped," Raven cried. "We'll be killed!"

"Shut up," Cale hissed, "and stay behind me."

He didn't have to ask twice. Raven was happy to put anything she could between her and the ferocious jaws and claws of the grizzly.

"Three Toes has a long memory," Cale said. "He won't have forgotten what happened the last time we tangled. Just don't move."

"You *know* this bear?" Raven asked incredulously.

"In a manner of speaking," Cale said. "He gave me this little souvenir last time we met." He reached down to draw his fingers across the claw marks on his chest. "I returned the favor, of course. Let's hope he thinks twice about repeating the experience. Best thing to do is call his bluff."

"You aren't scared of him?" Raven queried.

"Me? Scared?" he scoffed. "Naw."

He was lying. Raven had her arms around his waist from behind, so she could feel the tension in him. He was only saying that so she wouldn't be afraid. There was danger, terrible danger, here.

Raven's first instinct was to run, but she realized Cale had kept her from making that fatal mistake. To run was to invite the bear to chase them. That could end only one way. Instead, Cale was challenging the bear, confronting it beast to beast. To her amazement, the bear backed down.

Three Toes dropped down on all fours and sauntered away into the forest.

Cale exhaled, a long deep breath of relief.

Raven snorted. "You stupid, foolish man. To face a bear unarmed! That was a crazy thing to do!"

"What choice did I have?" he snapped back. "I knew what I was doing, Raven."

"But to be caught without a weapon —"

"I was taking a damned bath!" Because she had said he stunk. Or at least, insinuated it. "I agree, taking a bath was an idiotic thing to do. You won't find me making that mistake again!" And if he stank to high heaven, that was her tough luck!

Cale would have stomped out of the water, except the rocks on the bottom hurt his tender feet. He was forced to mince his way back to his clothes.

"You cannot put those filthy clothes back on!" Raven cried in alarm.

"They're all I've got," he said through gritted teeth. "You just burned the rest!"

Raven watched in dismay as he yanked on the dirty long johns and pulled on the blood-stained shirt. On top of that he added the bearskin coat.

The beast was back.

Cale picked up his Hawken which, she now realized, had never been far from hand, and marched up the hill toward the cabin.

He hadn't gone any great distance before he stopped abruptly. He turned and scowled at her. "Are you coming? Or are you going to stand there and wait for

Three Toes to come visiting again?"

Raven made her way to the edge of the creek and sat down to slip on her moccasins. She felt Cale's angry gaze as she gathered up the dishes he had washed and started up the hill after him.

"The clothes I burned were rat-bitten," she said to his back, in an effort to assuage his fury.

He halted in his tracks and turned to confront her. "If I didn't care, why should you?"

"I plan to make new ones," she retorted, her temper mounting.

"With what?" he demanded. "I haven't got any flannel for long johns."

"I thought you could bring me deer-skins —"

"Looks like you've got my whole damned life planned for the next couple of months," Cale said with a snort of disgust.

He started marching toward the cabin again. When he reached the door he stopped to wait for her. "Get on inside."

He could see she was losing her hold on the dishes. Any second they were going to tumble into the dirt. He reached out and grabbed a few of the ones teetering on top of the stack.

"Get on inside," he repeated.

He hadn't planned on coming inside with her. He needed time alone to think. But he couldn't very well toss the dishes in after her, so he followed her into the cabin.

He dropped the dishes on the table and barely caught a tin cup that rolled toward the edge.

"I can make you some coffee now," Raven offered.

It was obviously a peace offering, but he wasn't sure he ought to take it. He looked around the cabin, which had suddenly shrunk in size with the two of them inside it, and decided it was way too small for the both of them. Especially when one person didn't much like the other.

Only, what if she had liked him a little better? Now that he was clean, he thought of putting his skin next to hers. Something of what he was thinking must have shown on his face, because her eyes suddenly grew wary.

He wanted her. He could have her if he took her by force. From her previous attack on him, he knew she would fight him, but she was small, and he could overwhelm her in the end.

Suddenly Cale knew he couldn't stay here another minute, in the cabin she had made too much like a home, with a woman

82

he wanted but wasn't willing to take by force. He needed time to think, time to plan what he was going to do. But there was no earthly reason for him to be leaving his cabin. He had just gotten home!

Only she had given him a reason. And she could hardly complain that he was leaving if he was only doing her bidding.

"Forget the coffee," he said. "I've got to go."

He felt immeasurable satisfaction at the stunned look on her face. "Go? Where?"

His lips curled in a wry smile. "Hunting. You asked for deerskins. I'm going to oblige you."

"How long will you be gone?"

"As long as it takes." Cale didn't know himself how long it was going to take him to figure out what to do about Raven. She had turned his whole life upside down, and he wanted time to sort things out on his own.

"It is not necessary to go far, is it?" she asked. "Or to be gone very long."

He had his mouth open to say he wouldn't go at all if she was afraid to be left alone. But he felt an invisible noose tightening around his neck. Before he could change his mind he said, "How far I go and how long I'm gone is my business. I don't owe you any explanations."

"But —"

He felt a part of himself surrendering to the anxiety in her eyes. He was on the verge of relenting, of staying to keep her company. There was another part of him that still chafed from the knowledge that he was no longer all alone. That after ten years as a solitary man, there was someone for whom he was responsible and to whom he had to answer. The thought both terrified and infuriated him.

"Let's get something straight right now," he said. "I'm the one in charge around here. You do as you're told, and you don't ask questions. I decide where I'll go and when and how long I'll stay gone. Is that clear?"

"Go!" she said. "Go! I do not need you here. I do not care if you ever return! I can take care of myself!"

Cale stared at Raven. Her chin was up-thrust, her eyes lit with fire, her whole body poised in a stance of defiance. Her finger pointed him out the door. It was plain she didn't need him around. He must have mistaken the troubled look in her eyes. Well, so be it. If she wanted him gone, he was damned glad to accommodate her.

"I'll just get a few things I need, and I'll be out of here." He wasn't even sure what he was grabbing. He was still too agitated.

A mile away it dawned on him that he had been kicked out of his own house.

Cale wasn't sure where he was when he woke. He smelled coffee, though, so he figured he must've found company. Or company had found him.

" 'Bout time you woke up," a deep voice said.

"Laidlaw." Cale rubbed the sleep from his eyes and yawned.

He had shot three deer the day he left. He could have gone back home that same night. Only his pride wouldn't let him. He figured he would give Raven time alone to stew. Then maybe she would be a little more grateful for his company when he returned.

Every night as he had made himself a pallet on the cold hard ground, he had promised himself he would go home the next morning. And every morning he awoke determined to stay away for at least a month. It was becoming a damned matter of honor.

"Thought you'd be tucked up in bed all right and tight with that Injun squaw,"

Laidlaw said. "What're you doing down here roaming around the valley?"

Cale stretched out the kinks another night on the ground had put in his muscles. "I left," he said flatly.

Laidlaw laughed. "Threw you out, huh?"

Cale grimaced. "I told you I *left*."

"Yeah. And I'm Julius Caesar."

"Damned woman was obsessed with cleaning," Cale complained. "Washing dishes. Sweeping. Throwing things out. *Burning* stuff!"

"That's a woman for you," Laidlaw said. "Nest builders, every one."

"I already had my nest feathered the way I wanted it," Cale muttered.

"How long you been gone?"

"A week," Cale admitted. A week of nights spent dreaming about a woman with dark eyes and shiny black hair. A week of days spent feeling the softness of her hands against his flesh. A week of regrets for his foolish pride.

"What have you been doing with yourself?" Laidlaw asked. "Why didn't you come back to the rendezvous? There was enough whiskey around to float a canoe, horse races, arm wrestling. Rip-roaring good fun. Only broke up yesterday. We could have raised the roof together."

86

"I wanted to be alone."

"Missed her, huh?"

"I didn't say that!" Cale snapped.

"See it on your face," Laidlaw said philosophically. "You're wound up tight as a bowstring. Only one thing does that to a man. You need a woman. Bad."

"I don't need her," Cale retorted. "Damned if I do!"

Laidlaw squinted at the low, dark gray clouds that scudded just across the tips of an ancient forest of fir and lodgepole pine. "Gonna rain, I think." He tightened his horsehair coat — the one he had made from the skin of his favorite gelding when it was killed in a fight with a mountain lion. "Stay here, and you're going to get a real dousing."

"I don't care," Cale said stubbornly.

"You planning to find another place to spend the winter?"

"Her father's coming to get her when the first snow falls," Cale said sullenly.

"Too bad."

"You want to come hole up with me?" Cale asked.

Laidlaw laughed, a deep guffaw that came up from his belly. "Never thought I'd see you scared. And of a woman!"

"I'm not scared! I just thought —"

Laidlaw shook his head to cut off Cale's flimsy excuses. "You're going to have to face her sooner or later."

"Damned woman stiffens like a board when I get near her. Threatened to cut me up if I touched her." Cale was appalled at how much his need for Raven escaped in his voice.

Laidlaw cocked a brow speculatively. "Are you telling me you don't know how to woo a woman into bed?"

Cale felt the telltale heat under his skin. "I know how. Doesn't mean I want to."

"You want to," Laidlaw said with certainty. "Woman's gotta be made to feel like sleeping with a man's her own idea. Then she's happy as a bee in clover."

"I'm not sure I can wait that long," Cale admitted in a quiet voice. "I'm afraid . . . I might do something I'd be sorry for later."

Laidlaw shook his head. "You aren't the kind of man who hurts something weaker than himself."

Cale's eyes hooded. "Once I would have agreed with you. Where Raven's concerned . . . I'm not sure of anything."

"I've got faith in you."

Cale snickered. "That's a comfort." He reached for the coffeepot and ended up wrenching his barely healed stab wound.

He drew back and worked the sore muscle by rolling his shoulder. He had yanked the stitches out himself, wishing the whole time for Raven's gentle touch. *Damn it, I miss her!*

Cale hadn't realized he had spoken aloud until he saw the cheeky grin on Laidlaw's face. He scowled. "I want her," he admitted. "I haven't had a woman in a long time."

As if any woman would do. Cale knew good and well there was only one woman he wanted. She had dark eyes and hair the shiny black of a raven's wing, and she was waiting for him in his very own cabin up the mountain.

"With your luck, she won't even be there when you get back," Laidlaw said.

Cale froze. The thought had never even crossed his mind. Or rather, he hadn't allowed it to cross his mind. Raven had agreed to the bargain. And, after all, she had the whole damned cabin to herself, along with all of his supplies. Why would she want to leave? He felt a cold terror at the very idea.

"Hey," Laidlaw said. "I was kidding."

Cale had already torn his ground cloth off the bed of pine boughs and was shoving it into his saddlebags. He grabbed things from the makeshift camp and packed without regard to neatness.

"Can't you stay for a cup of coffee?" Laidlaw asked.

"I've been gone too long already," Cale said. "I have to get back. Help yourself. I'll leave the pot."

"So long," Laidlaw said, clearly amused at Cale's headlong flight. "I'll see you at the next rendezvous."

Cale didn't even wave goodbye as he headed up the mountain toward his cabin. As he rode, he thought of all the things that could have happened to Raven. If she had stayed, that is. Three Toes might have come hunting berries and caught her unawares. There were Blackfoot and Arikara roaming the hills. She might have hurt herself chopping wood. Or slipped and fallen and broken her leg.

His mind created horrors he wouldn't have believed in a more rational state. But there was nothing logical about his need to return to the cabin. He was a lemming headed over a cliff into the sea. Raven was his. Pride didn't matter any more. Nothing mattered except getting back to her.

Raven hadn't worried at first when Cale didn't return. When her father was sulking, he always wanted to be alone. When a full week passed and Cale still hadn't returned, Raven had cause to wish back the words she had flung at him, to wish that she had left his dirty old cabin the way it was and not gotten him so upset.

She had never been completely alone before.

On the one hand, it was lovely to be able to sleep past dawn if she wanted, to wait well into the morning before breaking her fast. It was wonderful to be able to do exactly what she wanted, when she wanted. She took advantage of the opportunity to explore the open area around Cale's cabin. She found a tiny meadow dotted with an abundance of wildflowers, including lupine and Indian paintbrush and fireweed and late-blooming primrose.

Beyond the meadow, a virgin forest of fir and pine and aspen loomed high above her. The wind in the trees sounded like the exhale of some great beast. It made her shiver when she listened at night. And reminded her of another beast that growled when he was angry.

Raven wasn't afraid to be alone, but she was a little lonely. For the first time in her life there was nothing she needed to do. It gave her a chance to sit and think. She had known for a long time that she would never have a home or a husband or children. She knew her father would never allow it. But that didn't mean she hadn't dreamed of those things.

Since the time she was old enough to bear children, she had imagined herself with a husband whose eyes glowed with love for her, watching as she suckled a babe at her breast. Sometimes — before Ribbon Jack — when she had seen a white man look at her with admiring eyes, she had imagined what it would be like if he courted her, if he married her and took her to live in a wooden cabin like the one she had seen as a child.

But the admiration had always turned to lechery. And after Ribbon Jack, no white man had looked at her with anything except fear and loathing. No man, that is, except Cale Landry.

To her chagrin, Raven had begun to weave dreams around the man, despite his bestial looks, despite his bear-like behavior. She pictured them living in his cabin, with their children playing outside.

But the picture wouldn't stay in focus. Because it *was* a dream. Because being with Cale was only temporary, until she had paid her father's debt. And there was no love in his eyes when he looked at her, only lust.

And loneliness.

She didn't forget the loneliness. It made him vulnerable. It kept him from being, in fact, a beast. It made him human.

Raven pondered why she felt differently toward Cale than she had toward any other man. Even when she had dreamed of a husband, he had been a sort of protective figure who watched over her, nothing more. She had never dreamed of joining with a man, even though that was necessary to create the child in her dreams. It seemed strange to her that she should want to couple with Cale, but she did.

His face was not particularly attractive. Actually, she had never seen the face hidden beneath his thick black beard. She had a fervent desire to see it, though. His nose had a bump at the bridge where it had been broken and healed crookedly, but it was otherwise straight and not too large. His teeth were good and mostly straight. She imagined they would make quite a splash of white if he ever smiled. So far she had only seen him bare them in pain.

His mouth was hidden by his beard, but she had seen his lips flattened in disgust. The lower lip seemed more full than the upper, but that could be an illusion created by his mustache. His eyes were deep black wells where fierce emotion often surfaced. She liked his eyes.

His body was powerful, his hands large and callused, his legs long and muscular. She could not find fault with any of them. In fact, she already knew that touching him was pleasurable. But she had been given too little chance to let her fingers roam. She wondered what would have happened if they hadn't been interrupted by Three Toes.

On the other hand, it was probably a good thing the bear had shown up.

Raven had a dreadful fear that, once in the throes of sexual fever, Cale might turn into the sort of wild-eyed, brutal animal Ribbon Jack had been. She had no other experience with a man. She knew that beasts in rut would fight to the death to secure a mate. She had seen for herself the wild light in Ribbon Jack's eyes as he tore at her clothes and clawed at her flesh. She had writhed with excruciating pain as her body resisted his penetration. If she had not reached her knife in time, Raven knew he would have torn her in half with the sword he had wielded so unmercifully. What if the same thing happened with Cale?

She didn't trust Cale enough . . . yet . . . to believe he would not turn into a ravening beast. So her dreams were going to have to remain dreams, until the man returned to prove himself one way or the other.

Assuming, of course, that he did return.

Raven had begun to doubt he would. She put her dreams aside and headed back toward the cabin. It, at least, was real. She had made it as nearly into the home of her dreams as she could. It was a pity that when the first snow fell, she was going to have to leave it.

Seven

Cale didn't recognize his cabin. It had changed, like a plain green caterpillar into a spectacular butterfly. Where before there had been clutter, now neatness reigned. His traps and stretching hoops hung from pegs on the wall. The bed was neatly made up with a quilt that had been laundered so the pattern was visible again, the mattress stuffed plump as a partridge with fresh grass. The plank floor had been scrubbed clean. The potbellied stove was burning, and delicious smells emanated from a Dutch oven on top of it.

Obviously Raven had taken advantage of his absence to make changes. Not all of them bad, he admitted. The shadows he had taken for granted had been banished. Sunlight streamed inside, revealing dust motes and, if he was not mistaken, a fresh hatch of mosquitoes. Raven had never returned the scraped skin to the window, apparently preferring the fresh air and light

— and bugs — to the odors and gloom that had permeated the closed cabin.

Cale leaned over to sniff the wildflowers Raven had put in a canning jar on the table. The floral scent reminded him of her and made his groin tighten. Where was she? He knew she couldn't be far because there was food on the stove. He was chagrined to find everything so much in order. Apparently his race back to the cabin had been a fool's jaunt. She had managed just fine without him!

Cale dropped the pack he carried, which included three deerskins and about half the venison from the deer, which he had smoked. The rest he had eaten or left for the wolves. He resisted the urge to call out to her. He didn't want her thinking he had missed her. Even if he had.

On his ride back to the cabin, Cale had decided that, assuming he found Raven where he'd left her, he might as well enjoy her company. It beat to heck his other two choices: avoiding her or arguing with her. Remembering the beautifully crafted beadwork on her dress, he thought maybe he was going to fancy having a set of buckskins made for him. If the smells coming from the stove were anything to judge by, she could cook. And he already knew she had a real talent for cleaning.

"Hello."

Cale wheeled, surprised again by how silently Raven could move. He would have admired her for it, if he hadn't found it so disconcerting to be caught unawares.

"Welcome home."

It was amazing how powerful those two words were, what images they conjured in Cale's mind. A rocker by the fire. A hot meal on the table. A warm bed with a woman waiting for him. His throat tightened. Once upon a time he had expected all those things. Over the past ten years he had given up hope of ever having them. Now there was a woman in his cabin, and a bed and hot food on the stove. All he needed was the rocker, and he could make that himself if he set his mind to it.

Raven leaned down to pick up the three rolled deerskins. "Oh, you brought them after all."

"Did you think I wouldn't?"

She flashed him a quick grin. "I wasn't sure. You were so angry when you left . . ." Her voice faded, as though she were afraid that by mentioning his anger she would bring it back to life.

Over the past week Cale had moved past anger and frustration to acceptance. He was just going to make the best of a bad situation. From the looks of things, it wasn't going to be nearly so difficult as he had feared.

"Is there enough for me?" he asked, gesturing to the pot on the stove.

"You are hungry!" She dropped the deerskins and hurried to get plates to set on the table. "Take off your coat and make yourself comfortable," she urged.

Cale felt a rising irritation. It was his home. He ought to be the one offering her hospitality, instead of the other way around. He bit back the retort that was on his lips. *No arguing,* he told himself. He was determined to keep things on an even keel.

Raven dished up stew and set it on the table in front of him. She scooped up a bowl for herself and joined him, after pouring each of them a cup of coffee.

"The hunting was difficult?" she asked.

"I got all three deer the first day," Cale confessed.

"Then why . . ."

"I spent the rest of the week figuring out what to do about you."

Raven flushed. "I did not think you wanted anything to do with me."

"I made a mistake bringing you here, that's for sure."

99

The color that had so recently rushed to Raven's face fled, leaving her pale. "My father will not come until the first snowfall," she reminded him. "I have nowhere else to go."

Cale sighed. "I know. That's why I figured the best thing to do is for us to cry peace and be friends."

"You want to be my . . . friend?" Raven had never had many friends, and of the few she had, none of them were male. Her eyes narrowed suspiciously. "What does that mean, friends?"

"You know. Talk together, work together, play together."

"Sleep together?" Raven asked cautiously.

"Under the same roof," Cale said.

"But not in the same bed?"

"No," Cale said evenly. "Not in the same bed."

"But there is only one bed here," Raven pointed out.

Cale glanced over at his bed. She had her things set out all around it. Plainly, while he'd been gone, she had claimed it. His lips curled cynically. "I'll take the floor."

"All right."

She had agreed to that damn quick, Cale

100

thought. But why shouldn't she? He was the one who would end up on the cold, hard floor.

"Shall we shake on it?" Cale extended his hand across the table, wondering if she would dare to touch him. He saw the effort it took for Raven to place her hand in his. Her skin was soft, though the tips of her fingers were callused from hard work. She barely gripped his hand, and he returned the slight pressure before letting her go. She withdrew her hand quickly, and her grin flashed.

"Now we are friends," she said. "I shall make a buckskin shirt for my friend from the skins he has brought me."

"Is there something I could make for you?" Cale didn't know why he had offered, except he didn't want to be in her debt, and if she was going to make him a shirt, then he ought to do something for her in return.

She shook her head. "I need nothing. Only . . . only there is something you could do for me."

"What's that?"

"Would you read to me from your books? I have looked at the pictures in some of them, and I wish to know the story also. But I cannot read."

"Sure." Cale saw himself sitting in a rocker with her in his lap, her head snuggled under his chin and a book in front of them both. He shoved the image away. In the first place he didn't have a rocker. In the second place, she could barely stand to touch his hand, let alone sit in his lap. In the third place, he had no business dreaming about a woman who was only going to be around until the first snowfall.

She spent the afternoon outside working on the deer hide, scraping the skin to make it smooth. There were several more steps, she explained, before the skin would be ready, but she had made a start.

For a while Cale merely sat on the threshold of the cabin and watched her, marveling at the strength in hands that were so slim and feminine. Her hair blew freely in the wind, but she apparently tired of shoving it out of the way. He watched, entranced, as she quickly braided it in a single, silken tail that hung halfway down her back. Soon, beads of sweat appeared above her lip. He had the craziest urge to taste her skin, to lick away the salty drops.

That was when he decided it would be better not to watch her so closely. Not when he had declared they should be friends and had shaken on the deal.

He had wood to chop for the winter, and he figured the hard work would keep his mind off the girl. Cale spent the afternoon splitting pines and cutting them into manageable pieces. As he worked he couldn't let go of the thought that he could use some of the wood to make himself a rocker. Soon he had the rails for the back, then the slats for the seat and the legs. Finally he sat down to work on the curved rockers. By dusk, he had all the pieces cut out. It only remained to shape and smooth them and put them together.

Raven had noticed Cale's eyes on her, and it had made her feel a little frightened at first. What if he decided he wanted to do more than look? But he never made a move toward her. She snuck a peek at him once or twice, and saw that his eyes held only admiration. It was a look that made her feel warm inside. Or perhaps it was only the sunlight that made her wish she could bathe her face in the creek.

Raven noticed immediately when Cale left his seat by the door. He worked steadily with his ax, chopping with sure, steady strokes. Soon he had shed his shirt. The first time she raised her eyes and found herself staring at his bare chest she drew in a sharp breath. Her beast was a truly magnificent animal.

The scar where she had cut him was still pink, but his injury didn't seem to affect the smooth swing of the ax. His muscles flexed and relaxed as he worked. His strength and grace were impressive, and she had to force her eyes away from him and back to her work. She hadn't been looking at him with the eyes of a friend. Friends didn't want to touch the way she wanted to touch.

She consoled herself with the thought that she would have felt the same way if he had been a superb stallion. She would have wanted to confirm the supple beauty with her hands. It was safer, she decided, to keep her eyes and her hands to herself.

Raven hardly noticed the coming of dusk. She was so involved with what she was doing that she jerked unconsciously when she felt a touch on her shoulder.

"Cale!"

"Who did you think it was?" he asked, unable to keep the exasperation from his voice. She had jumped as though he'd scalded her. But he supposed that was to be expected, considering what she had been through with Ribbon Jack.

"I'm sorry," she said. "I forgot where I was. I know you would never — That is —"

"I'm not Ribbon Jack," he said flatly.

"No," she said faintly.

He wished now he had killed the man. He had been a fool to feel the least bit sorry for someone who had left such shadows in an innocent woman's eyes. Cale tried to make himself look less threatening, but he didn't know how. He was big. He was strong. There was no changing that. But he held out a hand to her palm up, submitting his great size and strength to her will.

"It's time for supper," he said. "Shall we go inside?"

He felt a tightness in his chest when she reached out and took his hand. He could see from the look in her eyes what courage it took for her to reach out to him. He shook inside when he thought of how fragile she was, and how easily he could hurt her. Not that he would. But it was clear now, if it hadn't been before, that she was a person with feelings — and fears — that would have to be dealt with.

She allowed him to help her to her feet, but freed herself to gather her work. He busied himself putting away his ax, then joined her in the house.

Raven had crossed some invisible hurdle when she took Cale's hand. He had offered it in friendship, and she had accepted. She was willing to give him her trust — until he proved himself unworthy of it.

At the supper table, she found herself telling him what she had done to pass the time while he was gone, about the flowers she had found, and the time she had spent doing nothing at all.

He told her about meeting Laidlaw and the rendezvous breaking up and how he always looked forward to it and then after a day or so couldn't stand the crowds and had to leave.

"I like living alone," he confessed.

There was an embarrassed silence, while his words hung in the air. It was plain to Raven that she had intruded on his privacy. Even if it wasn't her fault. "My father will be coming —"

"I don't mind having you here," he cut her off. "I mean, I like living alone, but it's nice having company, too. A man gets tired of the silence." *A man gets lonely,* he thought, only he couldn't tell her that. Besides, he wasn't lonely with Raven around.

She managed a small smile. "Will you read to me tonight?"

He nodded. "Is there any particular book you want me to read from?"

She went to his bookshelf and pulled one out. "This one."

It was an illustrated edition of *Robinson Crusoe*. How apt that she had chosen the story of a man marooned alone on an island. It was a book that celebrated the strength of the human spirit, the ability of man to rise above adversity. It had kept Cale from going mad one winter when he had been snowed in for two months.

Cale pulled the lantern on the table closer, so he could see to read. He expected Raven to sit across from him, as she had at supper. Instead, she pulled her chair around to his side.

"I want to see the words when you say them," she said. "And look at the pictures."

She was closer to him than she had been all day. Close enough that he could see the way her lashes fanned out over her cheeks when she lowered her eyes. Close enough that he could see there were several freckles on her nose. Close enough that he could feel the warmth of her thigh next to his.

He read slowly and tried to make his voice rise and fall with the story. She was quiet in a way that reminded him of the reverence people have in church. She made little noises to punctuate the story, the only evidence he had that she was listening. He had no idea how long he read. He stopped when he felt his throat getting hoarse.

"That's enough for tonight," he said.

"Will you read again tomorrow?"

He took one look at her face, at the childlike expectation, and knew he would read again even if he croaked like a frog. "Of course," he said. "But I'm done in tonight."

It was bedtime. He settled himself on the buffalo hide in front of the fire, and covered himself with his bearskin coat. It wasn't comfortable, but he wasn't about to complain. He had made a deal, and he was sticking to it.

Raven saw Cale on the floor and knew she couldn't make him sleep there. He would be cold. And the floor was hard. If he had wanted to take advantage of her, he could have done it at any time. There was some risk in offering him a place on the bed, but she had decided earlier in the day to trust him. And it was a very big bed.

She took off her moccasins and slipped under the covers and over to the far side of the bed. "Cale," she whispered.

"Yes, Raven."

"There is room here for more than one," she said.

"I know."

"I would be willing to share with you."

Cale came up on one elbow. "Thanks, but no thanks. I can't guarantee that I won't roll into you during the night. I'd just as soon not end up with a knife in my ribs."

She pulled the knife from the sheath that never left her thigh and brought it out from under the covers. "You can take my knife," she said, holding it out to him. "If it will make you more comfortable."

Cale sat up, surprised by her generous offer, but still wary of accepting it. "Are you sure you want to do this?"

Raven nodded. "I am inviting you into this bed only to sleep. I . . . I trust you. We are friends, after all."

Cale took the knife from her and struck it into the wall beside her. "It's there if you feel you need it." He slipped under the covers beside her and blew out the lantern beside the bed.

After awhile he heard the steady breathing that meant she was asleep. It was a long time before he could get his own unruly body to relax.

Friends, he thought as he finally drifted

toward sleep. Cale had never had a friend that he wanted to hold in his arms and kiss and touch. It was a unique experience. He thought he could get to like it.

Raven woke in the middle of the night. Her hair was caught beneath Cale's shoulder, and she couldn't move her head. That was when she realized she was snuggled up next to him. Like most large animals, he was warm. She knew she ought to wake him and free herself. But then she would have to give up his warmth. Tomorrow morning would be soon enough for that.

If he tried to touch her . . . but she didn't think he would. After all, he had left her knife within easy reach. He was a strange man, her beast. Imagine wanting to be friends with a woman! She should be afraid of him, but she wasn't. Even this closeness did not raise the terror she had felt with Ribbon Jack. But then, it was not necessary to be afraid of a friend. It was a unique experience to be so comfortable with a man. She thought she might grow to like it.

Raven sighed and burrowed more deeply against Cale's side. He grunted, then shifted and slung an arm around her. She tensed for a moment, until she realized he was still asleep. Then she allowed slumber to claim her once more.

Cale kept his breathing steady, and didn't move a hair until Raven relaxed once more beside him. He had felt her awaken, felt her stiffen as she realized where she was. He had been ready for a knife in the ribs. Instead, her hand had slipped onto his chest, and her nose had burrowed into his shoulder.

He wanted very badly to kiss her, to touch her in all the places he could imagine touching a woman to bring her pleasure. But he wouldn't for the world have violated her trust in him. Maybe, with time, she would be able to accept him as more than a friend. She had to learn that he would never hurt her. He had to bide his time, and hope there was enough of it left before her father came to get her.

Cale shifted restlessly. He wasn't a patient man. However, he had learned over his ten years alone how to wait. The snow melted. Spring always came. But it couldn't be rushed. So it was with Raven. She would be his. Eventually.

He closed his eyes and thought about how Raven had looked sitting beside him at the table after supper. How the story had been so much more exciting with her listening, as though he were hearing it for the first time himself. It was too bad she couldn't read. Too bad he didn't have time to teach her.

Suddenly Cale realized what a bad bargain he had made with her father. It wasn't enough. A few months just wasn't enough. He wondered if the snow would fall early this year, stealing even the little time he had with her.

His arm tightened reflexively around her, and Raven made a grunting sound. He loosened his hold, and she sighed. He would be damned if he let her go. Orrin Schuyler owed him more than a few months of her service. The man had stolen a whole year's catch of furs! Cale had been besotted by a pretty face, and Orrin had taken advantage. He would have a talk with the old man when he showed up and would drive a better bargain.

Eight

It rained for a whole week, and the weather was colder than usual for summer. Cale put the skin back on the window temporarily to keep out the weather, but he made a point of lighting every lantern in the place. If Raven wanted light, she would have it.

She worked on the buckskin for his shirt, pulling it through rings that were smaller and smaller until it was smooth and supple and the color of butter. "Now I have to measure," she said, as she came toward him with a long string of rawhide. He held his breath, letting her check the length of his arms and the breadth of his chest and the distance from his nape to his buttocks. She looked adorable with her tongue caught between her teeth. It was all he could do to resist kissing her.

"When will it be done?" he asked.

"I can sew the pieces together and cut the fringe in a day or two," she said. "But the beadwork will take longer."

"You're going to decorate my shirt? What design will you use?"

"I have not decided." An impish smile curved her lips and she added, "Even if I had, I would not tell you. I want it to be a surprise."

He raised his brows. "I'm not so sure I like surprises."

"You'll like this one," she assured him.

Raven was amazed at her temerity with the gruff mountain man. Slowly but surely, as the days and nights passed and Cale kept his distance, she was losing her fear of him. More than that, she was growing to like him. He could be bristly at times, but even when he was angry she never felt herself in danger. She began to let herself dream about what it might be like if they lived here forever, if he took her for his wife and planted his seed inside her.

She was still afraid to lie with him, but she began to believe she might overcome even that fear, if only she had time enough with Cale before her father came to get her. If Cale would only give her some indication that he wanted her to stay, she would defy her father. But he never said a word one way or the other.

For a week Raven had watched Cale making something out of the pieces of wood he had cut the day he returned to the cabin, but she couldn't figure out what it was. She pointed to the curved piece of wood in Cale's hands and asked, "What are you making?"

"It's a rocker." He set down the bottom rail of the rocker and showed her how the chair would move.

She looked at him quizzically. "Why would anyone want to sit in a chair that will not stay still?"

His lip curled in a wry smile. "You'd have to sit in one to understand," he said. "It's soothing. Like being on a limb swaying in the breeze."

"I would be worried about falling off," she said tartly.

"That's why we sit on a rocker, instead," he said with a grin. "It isn't going to dump you on the floor unexpectedly."

"It seems like a stupid thing to me," she said.

"Just wait," he said. "And see."

The day Cale finished his rocker he invited Raven to be the first to sit in it.

She shook her head. "You go first."

He sat down, leaned back and gave the rocker a push with his toe. It creaked against the wooden floor. The rhythmic sound was as soothing to his ears as the rocking was to his body. He closed his eyes and took himself back to a time when he had lived in Virginia and his parents had each sat in a rocker on the front porch of their plantation. He wasn't aware of the smile that formed on his face, but apparently Raven was.

"I'm ready to try now," she said.

Cale got up and held the chair still while she sat down very gingerly.

"You can let go." Raven shoved with her toe and the rocker began to move. She had a deathgrip on the arms of the chair until she realized she wasn't going to tumble out of it.

"I suspect this reminds us of when we were babies being rocked in the cradle," he mused.

"Indian babies aren't rocked in cradles," Raven said. "But sometimes a papoose in a backboard is tied to the limb of a tree, and the breeze will make it sway." She leaned back in the rocker and let it move her gently to-and-fro. "It must feel very much like this," she said in a dreamy voice.

"I can see I should have made two," Cale said ruefully.

Raven's eyes flashed open, and she would have leapt from the chair except

Cale put his hands on the arms and kept her captive.

"It's all right," he said. "You keep rocking. I can use it later."

"But —"

He brushed her cheek with the back of his hand. "I'm just glad you like it."

He saw her eyes widen as he caressed her, but she didn't try to escape. Not that he hadn't made it virtually impossible for her to do so. But there was no fear in her eyes, as there would have been if she had felt truly trapped. So maybe he was making progress after all.

"I like this . . . rocker," she said, "but you didn't make it for me."

He stepped back. "Didn't I? Well, we can always share it, you know."

"We can? How?"

"Stand up," he said, backing away to give her room.

She stood obediently, and he sat down in the chair.

Her hands shot to her hips. "You have a strange way of sharing, my beast."

Cale grinned and held out his arms. "You can sit on my lap."

She shook her head. "The rocker will break. I have work to do outside," she said.

She was gone before he could offer the chair back to her.

He read to her every night at the table. She still didn't completely trust the rocker. The way she didn't yet trust him. *Someday,* he thought. *Someday she'll want to sit there with me.*

But the days were passing more quickly than he would have liked. He watched every move Raven made, felt his heart thump wildly when she was near. But he didn't make a move toward her that was the least bit sexually threatening, even though he often lay wide awake for hours after she had fallen asleep in the bed beside him.

Cale was amazed at Raven's patience with the tiny beads she was sewing on his shirt. She wouldn't let him see what she was doing, but it pleased him to sit in his rocker and watch her in front of the fire, her head bowed, intent on her work. He caught her rubbing her neck one night and lowered himself onto the floor behind her. He laid his hands on her shoulders, which tensed at his touch.

"May I?" he said.

She nodded.

He had never been so conscious of his

118

strength or the size of his hands. He moved her hair out of the way, exposing the skin at her nape. He was as gentle as he knew how to be, as he massaged her aching shoulders. She sighed once, and he heard another sound of satisfaction deep in her throat as his fingers pressed against her flesh. He watched her set the shirt aside, and her hands, for once, lay idle in her lap.

He couldn't take his eyes off the skin at her nape. It looked soft and silky and utterly enticing. He lowered his head and pressed his lips lightly against her flesh. He felt the tremor that ran through her, saw her hands slide to her sides.

"Raven?" he whispered.

She turned and looked at him over her shoulder. Her dark eyes were liquid, not frightened, but watchful. Her lips were parted, her breath coming in shallow pants.

He could have kissed her. Could have done that and maybe more. But it wasn't what he wanted most. More than anything, he wanted to hold her in his arms.

He stood and picked her up and walked with her back to the rocker. He sat and settled her in his lap. She hid her face against his chest, and her fingers tightened on handfuls of his shirt. He didn't rock at first, just sat there, marveling at the wonder of having her there in his arms, where he had always imagined her.

Then he began to rock. The floor creaked under the chair. That, and the fire popping, and the rustle of the aspens outside were the only sounds to break the silence.

He held her like that until she fell asleep in his arms. He looked at her with his heart in his eyes. How had she come to mean so much to him? How was he going to let her go?

He managed to put her to bed without waking her and joined her there. He had made his dream come true. But for how long would it last? He had made a bargain with her father. He would have to give her back. Unless she wanted to stay. But why would she? What kind of life could he offer her? Cale held Raven gently in his arms as he fell into a troubled sleep.

Three days later, just before bedtime, Raven presented Cale with his shirt.

"It's a wolf!" he exclaimed, as he examined the intricate beadwork.

"A lone wolf," she agreed.

"He's howling at the moon," Cale observed.

"He's calling to his mate," she said quietly. "Asking her to join him on the hunt."

Raven wondered if Cale could read into her gift the message she was sending to him. *I will be your mate, Cale Landry. I will hunt with you.*

His fingers lovingly traced the beadwork, but he said only, "It's exquisite. Can I put it on?"

She forced a smile. "Of course. I made it for you to wear."

He yanked off his shirt and pulled on the buckskin. It fit him well at the shoulders and across the back, yet gave him room to move. "Thank you," he said. "Words can't express what I'm feeling right now."

For a moment Raven thought he was going to kiss her. She wondered if she would let him, but he drew back. She felt disappointed and realized that, ever since that night before the fire, she had wanted him to kiss her. More than that, she had wanted him to see her as his mate.

How foolish. He only wanted to bed her. She knew that. But it was not enough, and she would not settle for less. She wanted it all, the husband and the home and the children. So perhaps it was better that he had not kissed her. Her father would be

121

coming for her soon, and she would have to leave this cabin and Cale. Better not to leave her heart behind as well.

Nine

Being friends with a woman, Cale discovered, was damned hard work.

On a sunny, Indian summer day in mid-September, Raven talked him into taking a walk to gather the last of the wildflowers in the wood. He had never heard of doing anything so silly, but she held out her hand to him, and he took it.

"Come with me. We will be carefree for one day."

Before he knew it, he was on his way into the forest with the picnic she had packed for them carried in a burlap sack slung over his shoulder.

Cale was astounded at the number and variety of wildflowers they found. What was even more beautiful was the pleasure shining in Raven's eyes. A lump filled his throat from just looking at her. Another, even more obvious tightness rose somewhere else. He reminded himself they were friends and kept his hands to himself.

Later, after they had eaten, she invited him to lay his head in her lap and relax. When he was settled, Raven placed her cool fingertips on his brow and gently smoothed it as she talked of her life among the Nez Perce.

Cale was appalled at the hardship and deprivation she described.

"How could your father have left you with them so long?" he demanded. "Six years must have seemed forever to a six-year-old child. Did you mind leaving when your father finally came to get you?"

Raven's brow furrowed. "I did not wish to stay longer with my uncle. He was not kind to me. And I longed for adventure. I wanted to travel and see more of what was beyond the mountains."

"Was your wish fulfilled?"

"I saw more than I wished to see," she said in a bitter voice. "There is much hatred and cruelty in the world."

Her fingertips were laced in Cale's hair, and he reached up to draw her hand down and press her palm with his lips. "I'm sorry you've suffered from that hatred and cruelty," he said.

It was the first reference he had ever made to the incident with Ribbon Jack. Raven stiffened, and if he hadn't been holding her hand, he knew she would have pulled it away. Cale suddenly felt barriers between them that hadn't been there for weeks. He sought a way to bring them back down.

"Was there ever a man you wanted to uh . . . a man you wanted?" he finished hastily.

The sweetest smile curved her lips, and she twirled a lock of his hair on her finger. "Yes. One."

Cale experienced a stab of jealousy that surprised him. Curiosity goaded him to ask, "What was he like?"

She stared off into the distance, as though picturing him in her mind's eye. "He's tall and very strong-willed," she said. "He has eyes that see beyond the surface of things and a powerful spirit that can be gentle when there is need."

"He sounds like a saint."

She laughed, a tinkling, vibrating sound that worked its way down inside him, shattering walls that had stood for long years. "Oh, no. He is a very earthy man. I have often thought him more beastlike than human."

"How can you want a man like that?" Cale demanded.

She smiled enigmatically. "It is easy. When you . . ."

Cale thought she was about to say *love,* and his stomach turned about three flips. He didn't want her to love another man. He wanted her to love him. Well, hell, he could want a woman to love him even if he didn't love her back, couldn't he?

"What about you?" she asked, resuming the caress of his temples that was both soothing and exciting. "Was there ever a woman you thought to have for your own?"

Cale debated the wisdom of answering her question. He had never told anyone — except Laidlaw, when they were both drunk — about Charlotte Anderson. Maybe it was time he did.

"There was a woman back in Virginia," he said. "We were engaged to be married."

"What happened? Did she die?" Raven asked.

Cale snorted. "She chose another man instead."

"Foolish woman."

Raven's statement, scornful as it was of Charlotte's choice in men, did more than anything in ten years to assuage Cale's bruised pride.

"Has there been no other woman?" Raven asked.

"No." It had been a long and empty ten

years, Cale realized. He had fled after Charlotte's betrayal and found solace in the mountains. He hadn't once looked back, hadn't once questioned his decision to leave the world with its false women behind him. He had satisfied his sexual urges with the Indian women at the annual rendezvous who were willing to be paid for their favors, but he had not chosen another life mate. Charlotte's perfidy had taken a toll far greater than stolen pride and a broken heart. She had snatched away his chance at happiness with a woman.

Now, by a quirk of circumstance, he found himself with another woman who was slowly but surely stealing her way into his affections. Somehow Raven had become much more than just a friend. Only, this time around he would be more careful. This time he wouldn't give her his heart.

Cale realized he had been staring at Raven's mouth the whole time he had been thinking, wondering what it would taste like. He had waited long enough. He didn't allow himself time to change his mind, just curled a hand around her nape and drew her down as he lifted his head toward her. If she fought him. . . .

Their lips met somewhere in the middle,

just a touch, a fleeting taste of wonder and delight.

Cale felt his pulse pounding as he glided his tongue along the edge of her closed lips. She moaned softly as she opened her mouth, and he slipped his tongue inside. He slowly stroked her mouth, and she made a whimpering sound in her throat. Then her tongue sought his, and he felt his groin tighten with desire.

Cale wasn't sure who broke the kiss first, but he took a shuddering breath as their lips parted.

He had kissed her, and she had been willing.

Cale kissed her again, not as a friend, but as a lover. And yet, the kisses he shared with her were all the more pleasurable because he knew and liked the woman in his arms.

So this was kissing, Raven thought, stunned by the feelings Cale evoked. She had never imagined his mouth could be so soft, yet demanding. Or the surprising warmth and wetness of his tongue. Or the way her belly drew up tight as his tongue stroked in and out.

It wasn't physical fear that made her turn her head away to escape his kisses. It was the knowledge that she was very close to losing her soul to the beast. She wanted husband and hearth and children. Cale offered none of those things. Only this, the brief joining of man and woman, the coming together of friends. It took every resource she had to keep her heart safe from lips that persuaded her to surrender it.

When Cale reached for her mouth again, Raven didn't — couldn't — deny him. She let him kiss her. And she kissed him back. She felt herself yielding. If it hadn't been for his beard, she might have been lost. It was just bristly enough to be uncomfortable. That discomfort brought a measure of reason to what had become a devastating sensual experience. Raven sighed and put both hands to her pinkened face.

"Your beard tickles," she said with a breathy, half-delighted, half-frightened laugh. She wrinkled her nose. "And it scratches."

Cale sat up and rubbed the coarse hair that covered his face. "Do you want me to shave it off?" Where had that offer come from? He hated shaving. Living in the mountains alone gave him the excuse to avoid it.

"Would you?" she asked. "I have wondered how you would look without your

129

beard." Raven rose and put some distance between them. Cale read the signals she was sending and stayed where he was.

Raven took a deep breath and then another, and managed a crooked smile. "I think I will wait for another kiss until I see what you look like beneath that beard," she teased.

She began to gather up the remnants of their picnic. But before they went back she reached out to touch his arm. Her eyes were lowered demurely. Cale held his breath, waiting for her to speak.

"I like your kisses, Cale," she admitted in a soft voice. Then she turned and began walking back to the cabin.

Cale stared after her. He had been a little awed himself by the powerful feelings Raven had roused in him. He began to wonder whether it was fair to take what he wanted from her without giving anything in return.

He didn't shave right away. In fact, it took him a whole week to work up the courage. Even then, he went off alone to do the deed. When he returned, Raven stared at him as though he were a creature from the deep woods.

"Well?" he demanded. "What do you think?" He asked the question with bravado, unwilling to admit her opinion mattered.

Raven quickly covered the distance between them and put her hands on either side of his clean-shaven cheeks. It was a gesture of reverence, of great gentleness and — the word *love* leapt to mind. Cale stood still beneath her caress, but the earth moved beneath his feet. The world shifted on its axis, and he saw things in a whole new way. An immense realm of possibilities appeared before him, and Raven was a part of it all. What if he kept her with him? What if they spent the rest of their lives together?

"You are beautiful," she said. "Not a beast at all," she added under her breath.

He ignored the second half of her statement and focused on the first. Even that wasn't exactly the sort of compliment he had hoped for. What man wants to be *beautiful?*

"Beautiful?" he complained.

"Yes, beautiful." She nodded for emphasis. Her deep brown eyes glowed with approval that warmed a cold, bottomless place inside him.

This time *she* curved her hand around *his* nape and drew him down for a kiss. He slanted his mouth across hers, which was already open to him. His tongue stroked inside to be greeted by hers. Passion rose swift and strong, and his arms closed around her and pulled her tight against him, so that his hardened shaft was pressed against her belly. He reached for her breast and felt the weight of it soft and heavy in his hand. His thumb skimmed the crest, and her nipple pebbled beneath his touch.

Raven pulled away from him abruptly, and he let her go. She was panting, and her eyes showed white around the edges. He suspected she must be remembering what had happened with Ribbon Jack. It wasn't what he had already done to her that she feared, he deduced, but what was to come.

He reached out a hand to touch her and saw the courage it took for her to keep from flinching. He cupped her cheek in his callused hand, willing her to trust him. "I would never hurt you, Raven. Is this the first time. . . . Have you ever lain with a man?"

He was asking if Jack had raped her. He was asking if she had given herself to that other man — the one she had described in such glowing terms.

"You would be the first," she admitted in a soft, shy voice.

Cale felt the awesome weight of responsibility for assuaging her virgin fears, along with a heady joy. No other man had touched her. He would be the first to bring her to ecstasy, to put his seed inside her and claim her as his own.

But he would have to move carefully if he didn't want to frighten her. Raven was willing. He had seen the evidence of that. But she was also frightened. His seduction would have to be accomplished with gentleness and consideration. It was a new experience for Cale.

Not that he hadn't taken his time wooing Charlotte, but Charlotte had been years beyond Raven in experience before he even met her. And, he suddenly realized, he had never worried about Charlotte's feelings the way he worried about Raven's.

"Have I told you that I think you're beautiful, too?" he said to Raven.

A faint pink climbed her throat to her cheeks. "Do you think so?"

He bent his knees and tried looking into her eyes. She lowered her lids demurely. "I definitely think so."

Instead of laying her down under him, he made up a chore that took them out of the cabin. At the last moment, he had gotten cold feet. He was afraid that he

133

wouldn't be able to still her fears. That she might turn to stone in his arms, or become hysterical and fight him, thinking he was Ribbon Jack. He didn't think he could endure that.

He backed off. As the days passed, he saw the confusion in her eyes, but he didn't know how to explain his fear to her. Men were the strong ones. They weren't supposed to be afraid. Cale became the most avuncular of friends. That was the solution, he had decided. If she truly trusted him as a friend, she wouldn't be afraid. But, as he held their relationship in abeyance, he was conscious that time was running out.

With his beard and mustache gone, it had quickly become apparent that his hair was too long. Finally, that morning, he chopped it off, too. His efforts were rewarded when he presented himself to Raven. Her wide smile and gurgle of pleased laughter wrenched his insides with a torrent of need. It was hard not to touch her. He searched her eyes, looking for something; he wasn't sure what. And he found it. Willingness. Trust. They were there in full measure. His hands began to tremble, and he turned from her to regain a measure of calm.

She warmed water for him to shave with and sat at his elbow, avidly observing him as he removed the dark beard that had grown overnight.

"Don't you ever get tired of watching me do this?" he asked her.

"No," she said. "It reminds me you are not a beast, that you are a man."

He frowned. "Was there ever any question of that?"

She grinned back at him. "You *were* awfully hairy when I first met you."

Cale punished her by grabbing her up in his arms and nuzzling her with his bristly cheek. She giggled with delight and fought him — not much and not long — until his mouth found hers, and her laughter turned into a moan of pleasure. Their tongues mated as his hands found her breasts. She arched herself into him as he thrust his body against hers, teasing them both, taunting them both, with hints of what their ultimate joining might be like.

She surprised him by pushing his long john shirt up out of the way and sliding her hands up his belly to his ribs. Her fingertips traced the bones that protected his heart, giving pleasure and seeking it in return. He paused to stare at her.

"Does it not please you?" she asked, her eyes wary.

"It pleases me very much," he assured her. "I was only surprised because . . . well, because you've never done it before."

"But I have wanted to touch you," she said.

He saw from her lazy-lidded look that she was indeed enjoying herself. There was no fear in her eyes, no caution in what she was doing. So he had not been mistaken. He had earned her trust. The waiting was over at last. He felt such a burst of jubilation that it was all he could do not to shout aloud.

"Help yourself," he said with a lopsided grin. "Touch me all you want."

He hadn't dreamed, when he issued his invitation, that she would take him at his word. Or rather, he'd had no notion of what it was she really wanted to touch. Because before he could say Sam Jackrabbit, her hand slid down the front of him, across the bulge in his buckskins.

It felt so good he bit his lip to keep from groaning. She slid her hand back up and the groan slid out anyway. Was there anything that felt as good as a woman's hand on a man's body?

His fingers clutched her waist, where he

forced them to remain as she investigated his body thoroughly. She must be damned curious, he thought, to need so much touching to figure the whole business out. His eyes drifted closed as he focused all his attention on the feel of her hands, measuring the length of him, moving lower, seeking out the sac that drew up tight as her fingers closed around it.

Then her hand was gone, and his eyes opened to find her staring curiously at him.

"Did I hurt you?" she asked.

"No," he managed to grate out. "Why would you think that?"

"The look on your face . . ." She reached up to smooth a brow he hadn't realized was furrowed. "And your mouth," she said, suiting deed to word and tracing his lips with her fingertip. "It looked as though your teeth were clenched."

Cale didn't doubt that. It took every ounce of control he had not to lay her flat and take her right then and there. "What you were doing felt good," he admitted grudgingly. "It's hard for a man if he can't finish what he's started."

"Oh," she said.

But she didn't offer to help him out. She just backed herself right up and said, "I

137

need to go pick some wild onions."

She hurried out the door and didn't come back. He left the house shortly after her and didn't return for lunch.

He wasn't sure why she had fled. Maidenly shyness? Virginal fears? It had to be one or both, he thought. But neither were the reasons he had been keeping his distance. Those were fears he could handle. She had given him all the encouragement any man could need. He knew that when he returned to the cabin, she would be waiting for him.

It was late September. The aspens were turning gold and some had already lost their leaves. Their white trunks stood like beleaguered sentinels waiting for the first snowfall. The bull elk had begun to bugle their challenge, eager to fight for the right to mate with the females in their harem. The haunting, shrieking sound pierced the forest, heralding the onset of winter.

The first snowfall might come as soon as early October. Of course it would melt away; the snow usually didn't stay on the ground until late November. But Orrin had said he would come with the first snowfall. That could be a week from now, maybe two, but surely not longer than that. Cale knew he couldn't wait any longer.

Raven might never be totally unafraid. He was willing to take the chance that she was ready to be loved by him.

Tonight he would make Raven his.

Ten

Raven knew she had been playing with fire this morning. It was the heat that drew her close. In the past she had kept enough distance not to get burned, but now she wanted more. And she was willing to risk the flames for the ecstasy that all her teasing, titillating experiences with Cale had promised her she would find if she leapt into the inferno.

She had marveled anew each day when she saw the striking planes, the bold cheekbones and strong chin that emerged when Cale scraped away the dark growth of beard that had grown overnight. It was a strong, hawklike face, and she had lost her heart for good the moment she first saw it clean shaven.

Once, Raven had named the things about Cale that made him a lovable man. It was a very short, but significant list. Strong and brave, he was a man whom a woman could be proud of. He was a good hunter, and there was always meat for the table. He was not cruel.

On the other hand, he was not always gentle. Before he shaved each morning he looked the beast she had once believed him to be. He was stubborn and impatient. He wanted his own way and argued to get it. He had loved only one woman, and it appeared he would never love another.

Yet, she had fallen in love with him, true and deep and forever. Not only because of who he was, but also because of how he made her feel. Beautiful and desirable and cherished. To Cale she was special, an irreplaceable person, unique and individual. It was something she had never experienced before.

With the Nez Perce, she had merely been a child among many, welcomed when she arrived and dismissed when she was taken away again. To her father, she was a cheap and ready source of labor, an irritant at times and valued only because she could serve him. With Cale, she had the sense that if she were gone, there was no one else who could please him, who could tease him and taunt him and kiss him, in exactly the same way.

Raven never felt so much a person of worth as when she was with Cale. It was a feeling she liked, which she was loath to lose. Above all things, she wanted to mate with him. She knew he wanted her. She also knew that time was short for both of them.

This morning she had known for sure that making love to Cale would be worth the pain that would come when he broached her. She had overcome the terror of lying under a man who had the power to brutalize her. She supposed that meant she had learned to trust Cale. Because, although her fear was real, it was manageable. And Raven wanted a memory to take with her when she returned to her father.

Soon, the day would come when she would not see Cale again unless they happened to cross paths at a rendezvous. The comfortable home she had arranged for them in the cabin would be a memory. The children laughing and playing around them would remain a cherished dream.

Her chest ached when she thought of a lifetime without Cale. But her father would never willingly give her up, and she feared that, while Cale had welcomed her company for this brief time, he would be equally glad to return to the solitude he had treasured for the past ten years.

She glanced out the window and saw the first snowflakes falling. They were tiny and delicate, and she stuck her hand out through the open window to let them drift onto her skin. It was time to tack up the oiled animal skin that covered the window in bad weather, to shut out the snow, and with it, the light. The house would become dreary once more. When she left, she supposed Cale would revert to his old habits, and the cabin would smell of beaver and muskrat and man.

Raven felt a thickness in her throat that made it difficult to swallow. She forced her thoughts away from the future. There was still today. And tonight.

Raven wasn't sure how she knew that Cale planned to come to her tonight. From the looks that had passed between them before she had fled, by the kisses and touches, she knew the time had come. It would have happened this morning if she had not run away. Wild onions, indeed! She had picked enough to put in *ten* stews.

When she had returned to the house, Cale had been gone. Now it was nearly dusk. If he didn't return soon, he was going to get caught in the season's first snowstorm.

Raven busied herself tacking the oiled skin over the window. When she was done, she lit a lantern, even though it was still daylight, to keep the shadows at bay. She set the leftovers from the midday meal back on the stove. Cale would be hungry when he got back.

And cold.

Raven built up the fire until it was roaring. She stoked the potbellied stove so it radiated heat. With the window covered, it was almost toasty inside. She could no longer see her breath in the air.

He entered the house in a flurry of wind and snow-flakes, slamming the door shut and latching it behind him.

"It's colder than blue blazes out there."

"Give me your coat," Raven said.

Cale slipped the bearskin off his shoulders, and Raven hung it on a peg by the door.

Cale shook his head like a dog, flinging snowflakes off his hair and eyebrows. Some had already melted in the heat, and his face was covered with droplets of water. Raven grabbed a cloth and began dabbing him dry.

He stood silent under her ministrations, and it wasn't until she had no more excuse to touch his face that she realized his eyes, watching her, were avid with desire.

Raven didn't want to wait for supper or nightfall and maybe lose her courage.

"Cale," she said, tracing his eyebrow with her fingers. "Cale," she repeated as her fingertip found the slight bow in the center of his upper lip. His tongue dipped out and caught her unawares. She drew back with a startled laugh.

There was no humor in his eyes. Only a fierce, white-hot need that burned in the darkness.

"Raven," he said in a grating voice. "I . . ."

"Yes," she said. Only that one word.

But it was enough.

He caught her up in a crushing hug and found her mouth with his. His tongue thrust possessively, staking his claim. His hands roamed her back and one slid up to capture her head and keep her still for his kisses.

Raven moaned, a soughing sound deep in her throat as her body drew up tight. She returned Cale's kisses, parrying his thrusting tongue with her own, until she was gasping for breath and her whole body quivered with desire.

"I want you," he rasped. "I want to feel your skin. I want to touch you."

"Yes, Cale. Yes, please."

Then he was stripping her bare, and she was glad of the roaring fire that made it possible to stand before him naked and not be covered with goose flesh.

His eyes were heavy-lidded, his gaze fierce and possessive as he ravished her body without laying a hand on her.

Raven felt her nipples peak, and her heart pounded as Cale ignited a fire in her blood with his eyes.

"I want to see you, too." She took the two steps that put her within arm's reach and began to undress him. He didn't give her a chance to finish, quickly stripping himself until he stood naked before her. He was an intimidating sight, muscle and sinew and bone. And he was aroused, his shaft standing amid a nest of dark curls. She reached out to close her hand around him. He was warm and soft and hard all at the same time.

Cale gave a ragged sigh and slipped his hand between her legs to cup her dark curls in an equally intimate way. She gasped when he slid a finger inside her. Raven was astonished at how easily he had done it and how good it felt. She looked up and found his features taut with pleasure, his smile a little crooked, his eyes focused on her face.

"I want to say don't let go," he said as his smile broadened, "but I think if you

146

don't, this is all going to be over before it's started."

He removed his hand from its ultimate resting place and reached to free himself from her grasp. Raven released him with reluctance.

Cale lifted her into his arms and headed for the bed. "I think we'll be more comfortable here." He lay down beside her and stared at her without touching.

She felt shy under his perusal and would have covered herself except that his hand reached out to stop her.

"You're beautiful," he said. "Your nipples are such a rosy brown, and your skin is so smooth and pleasing to the touch." His hand stroked her body, his callused fingers rough against her silky skin. Her body quivered as he explored the underside of her breast, the shape of her ribs, the hollow of her belly, the backs of her knees. He left no spot untouched.

She took advantage of the opportunity he had given her to return the favor, feeling the washboard hardness of his belly and playing with the coarse curls on his chest. She was amazed to discover that his nipples peaked when she accidentally brushed them. She indulged herself by testing the texture of his skin with her lips.

She tasted the faint salty sweat and smelled the musky man-scent that was his alone.

"Raven, sweetheart," he murmured. "You're killing me."

She looked up and realized he wasn't anywhere near dead. "I want to touch," she said.

"Turn about's fair play."

She found herself flattened beneath him, with his hips caught in the cradle of her thighs, and then he slid down far enough to cup her breast with his hand and to close his mouth over the nipple.

He sucked.

She groaned and writhed.

Cale made a sound deep in his throat as Raven arched high and hard against his shaft. He shoved her knees apart with his legs and thrust quickly and surely, knowing where he wanted to be. Only he hadn't ever had a virgin before, and when he would have pressed home, he found the way blocked.

Raven cried out. "Cale! You're hurting me!"

Cale withdrew and rolled onto his back beside her. He covered his eyes with his arm and willed his body to stop its throbbing. He was panting, and took several deep breaths to catch up with his need for air.

Raven lay staring at the chinked log ceiling. She should have kept her mouth shut. She should have borne the pain in silence. Now look what had happened.

She glanced over and saw that Cale was no longer aroused, and when he caught her staring at him, he grunted and turned onto his side away from her.

"I'm sorry," he muttered.

"It is I who am sorry," she said in a quavery voice. "I . . . I did not know it would hurt so much."

"I didn't think it would either," he admitted with a shaky sigh.

"Do you want to try again?" she asked.

He rolled onto his back and then onto his side, facing her. "Do you?"

She nodded.

He sat up and pulled her into his lap. "We'll go slower this time," he promised. "I'll try to be gentle." He swallowed hard. "There will still be some pain. There's a barrier . . . I'll have to break through it."

She swallowed back the acid bile of fear. "It will be all right," she assured him, because she could see he needed the reassurance before he would touch her again.

"I . . ." He had been about to say *love,*

Cale realized with astonishment. It wasn't love he was feeling right now; it was gratitude for her sacrifice. He knew it was going to hurt her, yet he wanted pleasure to be part of their joining. So he was going to couple with her as gently as he could. To become a woman, she had to be broached. And better him, who cared for her pain, than some other man.

"All right," he said. "We'll try again."

Only this time Cale could feel there was none of the compliance in her body that had been there earlier. She was stiff and dry, and his task was a hundred times more difficult.

"You have to relax, Raven," he murmured.

"I am trying!"

He was tempted to give up then and there, but he knew it wasn't going to get any easier. So he took his hands off her and put them on the pillow on either side of her head and settled himself in the cradle of her thighs. Then, with his mouth alone, he began to woo her with kisses. Small, sweet kisses on her eyebrows and cheeks. He traced the shell of her ear with his tongue and was satisfied to feel her shiver.

He kissed one side of her mouth and

then the other and finally teased her lips open with his tongue. Then he began to mime the sex act with long, slow thrusts. He felt her body melting beneath his as the stiffness left her. Her hands found their way into the hair at his nape, and he felt his own passion rising.

Cale forced himself to tether his need, to hold his desire in abeyance while he concentrated on Raven. His hands formed fists as he forced himself to go slowly. His mouth moved from her throat to her collarbone and inched down to her breast, where he once again suckled a rosy nipple.

Her hands clutched at his shoulders, and her body began to undulate beneath him. He figured it was okay now to touch her with his hands. He started at her waist, with just a little pressure on either side, but one hand found its way up to cup a breast and shape it for his mouth, while the other forayed across her belly and down to tease the nest of curls between her legs.

He felt her tense and moved his hand away again, down to her soft inner thigh where the flesh was silky and warm against his callused fingertips.

He teased his way back up again until he found the tiny nubbin that he knew could bring her ecstasy. He was careful, soft and gentle as he had never been with another woman. Because he knew she was afraid. Because he wanted her to feel pleasure, not pain. Because he wanted her ready so she would never feel the thrust that finally made her his.

His mouth returned to hers and, as his fingers probed her, he could feel that she was slick and wet and ready. But he wanted her distracted. His hands sought out her breasts, and he caressed them and caught the nipples between his fingers with just enough pressure to cause a ripple of both pleasure and pain.

He took that moment to push himself a little way inside her.

He felt her stiffen and try to break their kiss, but he sucked hard on her lip and then slid his tongue along the underside of her upper lip until she gasped with delight and resumed the kiss.

With her hands clutched at his shoulders, her nails digging painful crescents in his skin, he thrust with all his might.

It was over quickly. He was through the barrier and sated to the hilt. He caught her cry of surprise and pain with his mouth, and held himself still, taut with need, until her body acclimated itself to his. He felt the slow easing of tension in her belly and thighs. He released her mouth to croon soothing words to ease her over the shock of his intrusion.

"Are you all right?" he asked at last.

"I feel . . . strange," she admitted.

"Does it hurt?"

She furrowed her brow as though she were considering the matter. "Not exactly. I feel . . . full."

It also felt right, Raven admitted to herself. It had hurt. She couldn't deny that. But the greatest pain was over now, and she instinctively knew that it was a passing thing, never to be endured again. Which gave her the courage to say, "Are you done now?"

Cale smiled. Then he laughed. "No, sweetheart. I'm not done." He sobered. "But if you want me to stop now, I will."

Raven had some idea of the sacrifice Cale would be making if he quit what he was doing. His body was rock hard, his muscles tense, his body poised for action. She was glad he had asked, but she wasn't about to stop now.

"I want to experience everything," she said.

"Everything?" he asked with a wolfish grin.

She smiled back. "Everything."

He moved slowly inside her. It was as exquisite as it was exciting. Raven sought out Cale's mouth and kissed him with all the feeling she had for him. He returned the pleasure.

As he moved inside her, as his fingertips caressed that special spot between her legs, Raven responded with increasing ardor. It was as though her body knew what it wanted and sought it out. Her breasts arched to his hands and mouth, and her hips drove upward to meet his thrusts.

She could feel the urge to do . . . something . . . to find . . . something, but she wasn't sure what it was.

Cale knew where he was going and wanted Raven there with him. He wanted her to feel everything he felt, the rising excitement, the need for release. So he teased her and taunted her and aroused her for far longer than he had ever done with another woman.

He was rewarded in his moment of extremity by feeling her convulse around him. It was something he had never felt before with a woman, something so powerful, so overwhelming, that he cried out with the tormenting pleasure of it.

Raven was caught in the throes of an ecstasy so profound it sucked the breath from her. She gasped for air as the blood pounded in her temples and her body squeezed and tightened around Cale, capturing him as he planted his seed in her. Then she was floating, her body not quite earthbound, and she realized she did not want to return to firm ground.

Cale rolled over and pulled her into his embrace, keeping her snug against him. Their sweat-slick bodies were chilling quickly, and he pulled the quilt up to cover them both. Before she could find the words to tell him about the powerful feelings she had experienced, he was asleep.

Raven didn't worry. There would be time enough when they woke to talk about what had happened between them. She looked forward to the exhilarating experience of making love to Cale again. She would turn to him and he would kiss her and it would happen. Only next time there would be no pain.

She snuggled under his arm and closed her eyes, confident for the moment of what the future held for them.

Sometime later, a sharp knock on the door woke them both. It was shoved open before they had time to do more than sit up in bed.

"Well, well," Orrin said. "What have we here? Two lovebirds, I see. Time's up, Cale. I want my daughter back."

Eleven

Cale rose from the bed like a menacing beast, heedless of his nakedness. "What the hell are you doing here?"

"First snowfall," Orrin said, whipping his hat against his thigh and brushing flakes from his hair. "I came to get my daughter. Seems like you two got along just fine." Orrin crossed to the stove and took a tin cup from a peg and helped himself to some coffee.

Cale dragged his long johns on over his feet, then added his buckskin trousers. He figured that made him decent enough for company.

The whole time he was thinking *It's too soon. I'm not ready to let her go.* Could he live the rest of his life without her? Could he go back to being alone?

No.

He heard his next words as though they were being spoken by someone else. "I've decided to keep Raven. I'll pay for her.

Name your price."

He ignored the gasp from the bed. Raven would be happier with him than with her father, he told himself. He would make sure she was. Only, how could he expect Orrin to set a price on her? There weren't enough furs in the territory to pay what she was worth.

"Whoa, there, son. Hold your horses. Who said I'd be willing to sell her?" Orrin demanded. "She's my flesh and blood. To tell the honest truth, the thought of selling her never crossed my mind."

Cale was stunned when he realized the gist of what Orrin had said, of what he himself had said. *Buying Raven? Selling Raven?* If anyone else had suggested such a thing, he would have flattened them. But it was different for him. He loved her. Furthermore, he was determined to have her, and that meant offering whatever it took to get Orrin to release her.

"I'll give you my catch for the next six months. Hell," he said, shoving a hand through his hair, "that isn't near enough, is it? I know she's worth far more." Cale bit his lip. You didn't tell a man how much you were willing to pay when you were trying to bargain with him. Only it didn't seem right, suddenly, bargaining for

Raven. How could he possibly measure her worth in monetary terms? Except, he didn't know how else to free her from her father.

Orrin's eyes narrowed speculatively. He slipped into a chair at the table. "Well now, son, I'll tell you, I didn't realize till Raven was gone just how much I need her to help me out. It was like losing my right arm to be without her."

Cale settled down across the table from Orrin to dicker in earnest. "I know you can't set a value on her in worldly goods. But I'd be willing to give you all of next year's catch to keep her with me."

"Now, son, I'm sorely tempted to take you up on that," Orrin said. "But a year's catch?" He made a *tsk*ing sound. "I'm afraid that wouldn't last me very long."

"I've got gold buried under this floor. Enough for you to hire someone to help you out. It wouldn't be the same as having Raven. Hell, I know that! She's worth more than all the furs and gold I've got or ever hope to have." Cale heard the desperation in his voice. "You have to take the money. You have to set her free."

I need her. I can't live without her.

Orrin shook his head. "I'd only gamble the gold away," he said. "I think I'll keep the girl. Come on, Raven. Get your things together. It's time to go."

Once upon a time Raven would have obeyed her father. She would have gone with him and never thought twice about it. But she had been listening to Cale, and his words were music to her ears.

You can't set a value on her in worldly goods.

She's worth more than all the furs or gold I've got.

Because of Cale she had allowed herself to dream. He had held her and cherished her as someone worthy of his respect and love. She had begun to see herself as a person with needs and desires she was entitled to fulfill.

"I think the choice of whether I go or stay should be up to me," she said.

Orrin gawked at her as though she had grown a second head.

"What did you say?" Cale asked. It had never occurred to him that Raven might want to leave him. Or that she might stay if he simply asked her to.

"It should be up to me what I do," Raven repeated.

Sometime during his conversation with Orrin, Raven had gotten dressed. She had never looked more lovely to Cale. Her cheeks were still flushed from sleep, her hair tousled from lovemaking. She stood with her shoulders back, her chin held high in that regal way that made him think he ought to bow to her. He was willing to do that, just as soon as they were alone, and press his head to her breast and wrap his arms around her waist and love her as she had never been loved before.

That is, if she gave him the chance. That is, if she didn't leave with her father. He understood now that she was entitled to that choice. He could never force her to stay against her will. If she wanted to go, he couldn't — wouldn't — stop her. He had meant what he said to her father. There was no price he would not pay to keep Raven with him. Except, how did you measure the worth of the woman you loved? He would do anything to ensure her happiness. Even if it meant helping her to leave him.

Of course, he wanted her to stay. But he hadn't asked a woman for anything in ten years. And he wasn't sure he could now. Pride was a terrible, awful burden for a man.

"The decision is yours," he said in a voice that sounded like a rusty gate. "I'll support whatever you choose. If you'd

161

rather go back to your people than stay with your father, I'll make sure he lets you go."

"Now look here, son —"

"Shut up, Orrin," Cale said.

Raven felt an awful, sinking feeling of defeat. Cale hadn't bothered asking whether she wanted to stay. He had simply assumed she would want to go. She stared at Cale with her heart in her eyes, willing him to speak, willing him to ask her to stay. She even considered telling him that she loved him. But it would be foolish to admit she loved Cale before he had voiced his love for her. He was never going to love another woman. Perhaps it was better this way.

She turned her back on the two men. "I will go back to the Nez Perce. It is where I belong."

Orrin snorted in disgust.

Cale heaved a long, heavy sigh. Raven had made her decision. He would have to abide by it and make sure that Orrin did, too. He would have to let her go.

The hell he would.

Cale was across the room in two strides. He grabbed Raven by the arm and whirled her around to face him. He caught her shoulders in a deathgrip and fixed her with a fierce look from dark, angry eyes.

The price of having her was higher than he had ever dreamed. But he realized, suddenly, it was one he was happy to pay. There was one thing he hadn't offered her, one last inducement to convince her to stay. He could offer himself. He could offer love.

"Don't go, Raven. I love you. I need you, and I want you to be my wife."

Raven stared at his beloved face, taut with worry. His eyes were anxious as he waited intently for her answer. Her heart was in her throat, making it hard to speak.

"You want to be my husband?" she asked. "To live here in this cabin and have children together?" It was her dream come true, and she held her breath, waiting for his answer.

"Yes. Yes, Raven. You'll sit in the rocker with a child at your breast and I'll make another rocker and sit beside you. We'll rock together until we're old and gray. Will you marry me, Raven?"

"This is very interesting," Orrin said.

"Shut up, Orrin," Cale repeated. His hands were trembling and he balled them into fists. "Well, Raven? The decision is up to you."

She smiled. "Oh, yes, Cale, I will marry you. I lo—"

"Now, hold on a minute," Orrin interrupted.

"Shut up, Orrin." Cale's eyes softened, his hands relaxed and his lips curved into an answering smile. "Now, what were you about to say, Raven?"

"I love you, Cale," she said. "I have for a very long time."

He kissed her, passionately and possessively. She was his woman, a pearl beyond price. Cale intended to make sure she never doubted it in all the years of their lives.

"This might not turn out so bad after all," Orrin finally said, a greedy, speculative gleam in his eyes. He rose and headed for the door. "Two's company, three's a crowd," he added with a wink at Cale. "I'll just be taking myself off."

"You do that." Cale kept Raven tucked beneath his arm, her hip pressed tightly against his.

"See you in the spring," Orrin said as he let himself out into the snow. "I'll be back then to hold my first grandchild."

Cale just growled at the old man.

"You will be welcome, Father," Raven replied.

Cale shoved the door closed and turned to lift Raven into his arms. He stalked toward the bed, a feral animal in possession of its quarry. There was no doubt in Raven's mind that Cale would take what he wanted from her, that he would mate with her and claim her as his own.

She smiled. He was the beast again, wild and dangerous. As he laid her on the bed with gentle care, her heart swelled with love for him. She sought his eyes and found them filled with a savage need that was barely leashed. She slid her hand into the shaggy hair at his nape and pulled his mouth down to meet hers in a kiss that was all the more powerful for its tenderness.

"I love you, Cale," she murmured against his lips.

"I love you, Raven," he snarled in reply.

Raven moaned as his lips found hers and claimed them.

The beast had found his beauty, and all was well.

The
Christmas
Baby

One

The killing has to stop, Emaline thought. Somehow, someone has to make it stop.

Nobody knew how the feud between the Winthrops and the Bentons had started. But for twenty years, since before the War Between the States, the town of Bitter Creek in Nolan County, Texas, had run red with the blood of both families. The most recent victims were five-year-old Sissy Benton and fourteen-year-old Rufus Winthrop. The two family patriarchs had called a week-long truce so they could bury the dead. The Bentons attended funeral services at the Bitter Creek Baptist Church in the morning. The Winthrops took over in the afternoon.

Emaline Winthrop had lost both a father and a younger brother to the feud. At twenty-two, she had spent nearly her entire life under the cloud of animosity that existed between the two families. For the past five years a particular plot of land had been the focus of hostilities. It was an idyllic spot where a stream rimmed with pecan and cypress trees crossed a pleasant grassy valley about two miles south of town. Both Winthrops and Bentons claimed possession of the land and, more importantly, the year-round source of water for their cattle.

Emaline sat in a back pew of the church mulling over a plan to end the fierce contest over those precious acres of land. She would never have a better opportunity to suggest her idea. Today she intended to confront the family patriarch, Jeremiah Winthrop, and see what he had to say.

Emaline moved to the edge of the crowd that surrounded Rufus's grave at the cemetery on the outskirts of Bitter Creek. Her eyes slid to a lone figure who stood vigil over yet another fresh grave. It was John Fleet, the town blacksmith. His daughter, Bethanne, had been a third victim of the cattle stampede through town that had killed Sissy Benton and Rufus Winthrop. Fleet's face looked ravaged, and Emaline tried to imagine the pain he must be suffering. His wife had died a year ago, and now he had lost his only child. There was no rallying clan to lend him comfort in his hour of need. He was grieving alone.

170

Emaline hesitated a moment before walking the twenty or so steps that took her to the huge man's side.

"Mr. Fleet?" she said quietly.

He turned to face her with red-rimmed brown eyes that seemed vacant of all feeling — until he recognized her. She recoiled at the virulent hatred that contorted his face when he spoke.

"What're you doing here?"

"I just thought you might need —"

"Get out of my sight! You Winthrops and Bentons have done enough."

"I only wanted —"

"I don't need your sympathy," he spat. "Will it bring back my Bethanne?" he said in an agonized voice. "Just go away and leave me alone."

Emaline fled, her heart wrenched by his pain, more convinced than ever that what she was about to do was right. The feud had to be stopped, not just for the sake of Winthrops and Bentons, but for the sake of everyone who lived in Bitter Creek.

After the funeral service for Rufus Winthrop, the clan gathered at the house of its patriarch for the wake. Emaline approached the elderly man, who was sitting in a rocker on his back porch with a heaped plate of food balanced on his knees.

"I need to speak with you, Jeremiah," she said.

Jeremiah spoke through a mouthful of food. "I'm listenin'."

"I have an idea. A way to end the feud."

Jeremiah stopped chewing and stared at her. He swallowed before he said, "Don't talk nonsense, girl. Been a lotta folks tried to stop the fightin'. Them Bentons just won't hear a word of it. Only way to end this feud is to kill 'em all, down to the last man, woman and child."

Emaline shivered at the venom in the old man's words. As she dropped to her knees beside him, the skirt of her eyelet lace-trimmed gingham dress billowed around her on the dusty wooden porch. "What if I could end the feud without any more bloodshed? Would you be willing to stop the killing? Would you make the men put down their guns?"

Jeremiah eyed her thoughtfully. "What fly's buzzin' in that brain of yours, missy?"

"The problem is that both Bentons and Winthrops need the water in the valley. Why can't we just offer to share it?"

"We done that, girl. Them Bentons said they own the land, and we have to pay them to use the water. Ain't meanin' to pay for what's ours!"

"I see." Emaline took a deep breath. "What if there were a way to establish that the land belonged to both Winthrops and Bentons equally? Would that solve the problem?"

"What're you gettin' at, girl? Speak up!"

Emaline grasped the arm of the rocker to steady herself. "What if a Benton and a Winthrop married and had a child? It would be half Benton and half Winthrop, right?"

"I suppose," Jeremiah conceded warily. "Only ain't no Winthrop nor Benton neither one gonna do such a thing."

Emaline ignored him and continued. "Say the disputed land was settled on their child. The land would have to belong to both families then, wouldn't it?"

Jeremiah opened his mouth to voice another objection, then snapped it shut. His eyes narrowed as he stared at Emaline. "You got someone particular in mind to marry a Benton?"

Emaline flushed. She didn't like the way Jeremiah was eyeing her. She was a single woman long past an age when most girls married. But she saw no reason to marry when her husband was likely to die from a bullet. She had no wish to raise children when they were bound to be slaughtered in a senseless feud. She had made the conscious choice not to look for a husband, although she knew there were those who blamed her lack of a husband on her appearance. She wasn't exactly the typical young miss.

Emaline was extraordinarily tall. She had long red hair that was a riot of curls, and her face — actually her whole body — was covered with freckles. She counted her striking blue eyes and good teeth as assets. But her nose and chin were only ordinary, assuming they could be spotted past her freckles. She had a meager bosom and slender hips. Worse, she was headstrong and opinionated, two traits considered not the least attractive in a woman.

Emaline had resigned herself long ago to being an old maid. Thus, Jeremiah's speculative gaze left her feeling decidedly uneasy. "I've only made the suggestion that a Benton and a Winthrop marry," she said. "I expect it would be up to the clan to decide who should make the sacrifice. Whoever volunteered would be doing something wonderful, something for the greater good of all," she finished breathlessly. "Assuming the wedding took place right away, the feud could possibly be ended forever by a baby born at Christmas."

Jeremiah set his plate aside. "This is

something needs talkin' 'bout right away, specially since we got everybody gathered in one spot."

Jeremiah raised his voice to get everyone's attention. Couples streamed out of the house and came from under the shade among the live oaks to gather around the back porch. "Emaline here has suggested a way to end the feud."

Agitated murmurs erupted from the crowd. Emaline felt her face flushing an uncomfortable red. Her blush was a mortifying thing she couldn't control. She countered the effect by lifting her chin and pretending she didn't know she looked like a boiled beet.

Jeremiah explained Emaline's plan in short, terse words.

"Who'd be stupid enough to marry a Benton?" someone shouted.

"Likely get murdered in the marriage bed!" another cried.

"Besides, how do we know them Bentons would agree to it?" still another argued.

"Why wouldn't they?" Emaline retorted. "It would end the killing. It would bring peace to Bitter Creek."

A hush descended on the crowd. Most people had lost hope that there would ever be an end to the feud. Emaline's idea had awoken in more than a few hearts a long-suppressed hunger for peace.

"Why not at least suggest the idea to the Bentons?" one woman said. "The worst that could happen is they'd say no."

"First we gotta be sure we have someone willing to marry a Benton," another woman said. "No sense getting our hopes up for nothing."

Emaline became conscious of Jeremiah's hooded eyes focused on her. Her pulse began to pound as her heart raced in panic toward her throat. She turned to the elder statesman of the Winthrop clan, her hands trembling. "No. Not me."

"Why not you?" Jeremiah said. "You're a spinster, long past the age of marriage. And it was your idea."

"I don't want to marry," Emaline protested. "And especially not a Benton."

"Why not?" Jeremiah demanded.

"I . . ." Because the Bentons had killed her father and brother. Because she hated them.

But that was the problem, wasn't it? The Bentons hated the Winthrops who hated the Bentons who hated the Winthrops. It was a neverending circle of enmity that led to death and more death. Someone had to break the cycle of violence. Someone had to be willing to forgive and forget.

Emaline looked out at the sea of faces. She saw aunts and uncles and cousins, grandmothers and grandfathers, brothers and sisters, sons and daughters. All of them were at risk so long as the feud continued. At least her idea offered hope for an end to the killing. If someone had to be the virgin sacrifice for the greater good of all, she supposed she was as likely a candidate as any other.

"If no one else is willing, I'll do it," Emaline conceded quietly.

There was a collective sigh from the crowd.

"No!" a male voice cried. "I won't let you do it, Emmy."

Emaline's older brother, Devlin, shoved his way past their relatives. He was even taller than she was, his body lean and lanky. He was blessed with hair a deep, rich auburn rather than red like hers, and his eyes were hazel instead of blue. Emaline had always envied his complete lack of freckles.

Devlin reached a spot two steps below where she stood on the porch and grabbed her hands in both of his. "You can't do it, Emmy," he said, his eyes locked earnestly with hers. "Who knows what kind of monster they'll choose to marry you?"

"I firmly believe the Bentons want peace as much as we do, Dev," she replied in a steady voice. "Whoever they choose will be making a sacrifice, too. It's bound to be someone who believes in peace as much as I do. For that reason alone, we're certain to deal well with each other."

Devlin walked up the two steps that separated them, so he could speak privately to his sister. His brow was furrowed with worry, and his face was pale. "Think what you'll be giving up," he hissed in her ear. "A chance to find a man to love, a man who loves you. Don't do it, Emmy! I don't think I could bear to lose you, too."

Emaline knew Devlin had suffered as much as she had from the loss of their father and brother. Devlin wasn't married either, and Emaline had often wondered if he had come to the same conclusion she had — that it was senseless to marry when one lived at the heart of such a violent world.

She laid a hand on her brother's arm. "I have to do it, Dev. Don't you see? It's our only hope. The killing has to stop."

She saw the struggle in Dev's features as he dealt with the enormity of what she was about to do.

"Emmy, I can't let you do it. I should be

the one —" He stopped himself, biting off what he was about to say. "If I volunteered —"

"Thank you, Dev," Emaline said. "I don't think I've ever been more proud to have you for my brother —"

"But you don't understand," he said in an agonized voice, interrupting her again. "I should be doing it instead of you. But I have to talk to . . . I mean I can't just do it without asking . . ."

Emaline managed a chuckle. "If it's this hard even to talk about marriage to a Benton, how are you going to go through with the deed? No, Dev," Emaline said. "It was my idea. I'm the one who should pay the consequences."

"Well, missy?" Jeremiah prodded. "What's it to be? Do I speak to Horace Benton or not?"

"Tell Horace that I'll marry whichever Benton man they choose."

There were no cheers, no excited exclamations. Everyone present had suffered too many disappointments to believe it could be this simple to end the feud. But they were willing to try. Emaline saw that as a hopeful sign.

"I won't do it!" Conn Benton declared

to the assembled Benton clan. "You can't make me do it!"

"No one's going to force you," Horace Benton said in a conciliatory voice. "But you're the most logical choice to marry a Winthrop woman. First of all, your land borders the contested property. Second, you've been a widower for long enough. It's time you got married again."

"But not to a Winthrop woman." God, how he hated all Winthrops! They had murdered his wife when she was pregnant with their first child. He could never forgive them for that. Now it seemed he had been selected to marry one of them, to take her to his bed and get a child by her. They were asking too much. How could he bear to look at another woman, especially a Winthrop, when all he could see as he closed his eyes each night was his beloved Josie lying dead in a pool of blood?

He felt a frail hand on his sleeve. "It's a chance for peace, Conn. It's a chance to stop the killing."

Conn looked into his mother's troubled eyes. She had lost a husband, two of her three sons, and a daughter-in-law to the feud. She despaired of losing Conn, who had been more reckless with his life in the two years since Josie's death. At first he hadn't wanted to live. Now he lived only to kill Winthrops.

Could he give up his need for vengeance for the sake of his clan? Could he agree to marry a woman he hated before he even met her? Could he lie with a Winthrop woman, put his seed in her, and watch it grow, and not loathe the product of their union?

"I have to think about it," Conn said at last.

"You don't have much time," Horace Benton replied. "The truce we agreed upon for the funerals lasts a week. The Winthrops want the wedding to be held before the truce is over."

"What happens then, I mean after the wedding?" Conn asked. "Does the truce continue, or what?"

"I suppose it must," Horace said thoughtfully, stroking his beard. "A lot will depend on you and the Winthrop woman, I suppose." Horace cleared his throat uncomfortably. "On how quickly you can get her with child."

There had been some discussion about that. Both Conn and his brothers had impregnated their wives in the first months they were married. He supposed that was responsible, in part, for his being chosen as

181

the sacrificial goat. He tried to imagine himself bedding a strange woman on his wedding night. What if she were ugly? What if she repulsed him? What if he could not . . .

Conn forced his thoughts away from failure. All women were the same in the dark, he thought grimly. He would manage to do his duty. That is, if he agreed to the insane proposition that had been made to him.

Horace cleared his throat again. "Well, Conn. I suppose there's nothing else to be said. If you won't do it —"

"I never said I wouldn't do it," Conn retorted. "I merely asked for some time —"

"There isn't any time," Horace said vehemently. "I need to give Jeremiah an answer this afternoon. Will you do it or not?"

Conn looked for some way to stall. "I want to meet the woman first," he said.

"What?"

"The Winthrop woman. I want to meet her before I agree to marry her."

"That sounds sensible," someone in the crowd said.

"In the church. At six o'clock," Conn said. "I'll give you an answer after I talk to her."

"I'll ask Jeremiah to bring the woman to

meet you. I don't think he'll object. So long as you're willing to give us an answer then."

"I've said I will," Conn replied irritably.

It didn't give him much time to consider — it was already after four — but Conn welcomed the respite. He wondered what kind of woman would agree to such a harebrained scheme. It wasn't going to work. But they would still be married when all was said and done. And likely hate each other's guts.

His mother cornered him before he could leave Horace's place. "Conn," she said, "I want a moment of your time."

Conn refused to meet his mother's gaze. She had a way of making him feel guilty even when he hadn't done anything wrong. "I'm in a hurry, Ma."

Hester Benton knew her son well. She knew the pain he had suffered and perceived his righteous anger. She had left him alone for the past two years and seen him grow more and more bitter, watched him lose the laughter that had always sparkled in his eyes. The time had come for her to interfere. She couldn't allow him to ignore this opportunity to set things right. Conn had never been a cruel man. He might hate the Winthrop woman when he married her, but he would not abuse her. Their union could end the horror of the past twenty years. And perhaps when Conn held his son or daughter in his arms, he would be able to let go of the past.

"You have to do it, Conn," she said in a quiet voice. "If not for your own sake, then for the sake of your nieces and nephews. Your brothers' children deserve to live in peace."

"It's too late for that, Ma."

"No, it's not," Hester argued. "The only thing preventing peace in Bitter Creek now is your stubbornness."

"They killed Josie." Conn swallowed over the thickness in his throat as he turned to meet his mother's loving gaze. "I can't forget that."

"You may never forget," Hester said, "but you can forgive, Conn. You can give peace a chance."

"I'll think about it, Ma," Conn replied as he tore himself free of the compassion in her eyes. It was all he was willing to promise.

Conn was at the church at half past five. He needed some sort of guidance, and he wasn't finding it within himself. He was astonished to discover the Winthrop woman

184

was there ahead of him. She whirled abruptly when she heard his bootsteps on the wooden floor.

Emaline was stunned at the sight of Conn Benton. She had never seen a man so handsome. They were totally mismatched, she realized, the ugly duckling and the beautiful swan. Except in size. Thank the Lord, he was taller than she was. His black hair was straight and a hank of it hung over his forehead. He had piercing, dark brown eyes and strong, blunt features. He was large enough to be intimidating, except she was used to holding her own with intimidating males.

Nevertheless, she felt a little breathless at the sight of him. "I didn't expect you so soon. I mean, I suppose you're the one who . . ." Her words trailed off as she stared at him, trying to imagine herself married to him.

"I am," Conn confirmed. "And you're the Winthrop woman?"

"I am." She thought of them lying next to each other, his skin warm and golden . . . hers garishly freckled. And blushed. An incredible red. Her chin tipped up an inch in response to the incredulous look on his face.

God Almighty! Conn thought. This was

the woman they proposed for him to marry? Lord, she was a long string bean! And redheaded! Conn didn't think he'd ever seen such bright red hair. She had it tied down at her nape with a green ribbon that matched her gingham dress, but it still curled every whichaway around her face. And freckles! He gave an inward groan when he thought of the child they were supposed to make together and how it would likely inherit her freckles. And no figure to speak of in that long span of female. There wasn't much he saw to her credit.

Except her eyes. They were wide and blue and utterly captivating. Then she smiled. Not a big smile, but enough to put a dimple in her cheek, and he felt the warmth of it all the way to the pit of his stomach. He steeled himself against feeling anything. She was a Winthrop.

"I don't know who thought up this blasted idea, but —"

"I did."

"What?"

"It was my idea."

"What were you thinking, woman?" Conn exploded. "Of all the cockeyed —"

"It isn't as crazy as you're making it sound," Emaline interrupted. "It will work."

"If they can find two people stupid enough to go through with a marriage," Conn muttered.

"There's nothing stupid about this idea," Emaline insisted in a voice that reverberated with feeling.

Conn could see she was set on the idea of this marriage working a miracle. Well, maybe he could change her mind. He stalked down the aisle of the church to where she was, expecting her to back away. She stood her ground, and when he stopped a foot from her, he found her eyes only an inch or two lower than his own. He took a stance with his legs spread wide and settled fisted hands on his hips.

"Look, lady —"

"My name is Emaline. Emaline Winthrop. What's yours?"

"Conn Benton. Look, Emaline —"

"My friends call me Emmy."

"I'm not your friend," Conn said in a hard voice. "And I'll never be your friend," he added. "I hate Winthrops. I'll always hate Winthrops."

"And I hate Bentons," Emaline retorted. "What does that have to do with anything?"

Conn stood with his mouth open, but no sound came out. His brow furrowed. She was about the sassiest woman he'd ever met. She kept interrupting him, and she didn't look the least bit intimidated by his presence. But then he hadn't met many Winthrop women. Maybe they were all like this. "You hate Bentons?"

"Of course," she said in a cold voice. "They killed my father. And my younger brother."

"Then why did you come up with this cork-brained idea?"

"Because I don't want to see any more killing. I have one brother left. I want to see him live to a ripe old age. And I have aunts and uncles and cousins. I'd do any-thing to put an end to this awful feud. Even marry you!"

Conn didn't bother acknowledging the insult. She had reason to despise him. He was a Benton. Which was why he had to talk her out of this outrageous scheme.

"Have you thought about what we'll have to do?" Conn said, his eyes gliding over her intimately. "What the terms of this agreement involve?"

Her lashes lowered, and she turned red enough to wash out her freckles. "I know I'll have to come to your bed," she said quietly.

The slightly raspy sound of her voice

glided sensuously over him and sent shivers down his spine. "They'll want us to keep trying till you're pregnant," he said flatly.

"I know." It was almost a whisper. "I never wanted to bring a child into this world before," she confessed. "But to have a baby and know it can grow up in peace . . ."

Conn felt a band tighten around his chest. If there had been peace, he would never have lost Josie. "I don't want a wife. I don't want to marry again."

Her body jerked as though she had been slapped, and her startled blue eyes sought his face. "You were married before?"

"My wife was killed by Winthrops."

"I'm so sorry."

"Save your sympathy," he snarled. "This is impossible! I won't do it!" He turned, intending to march back down the aisle toward the door to the church, but she grasped his arm and tugged at him to stop. He whirled to brush her off, and she collided with him. He had thought her rather flat-chested, but definite breasts pillowed against his chest. Because she was so tall, their bodies fit together surprisingly well. Her hair, those riotous, flyaway curls, tickled his throat.

His body roused at the feel of her, and there was nothing he could do to stop it. He could only regret it. He didn't want to feel anything. He had been faithful to Josie's memory. He hadn't wanted a woman, and when he had needed one, he had forced himself to work until fatigue made the need go away. It was just that Emaline Winthrop had caught him by surprise. She felt soft and feminine. His body had recognized the shape of her and responded.

His arms had closed around her to keep them both from falling, and he noticed she was reed slim, where Josie had been rounder, her breasts and hips more womanly. And Josie's head had barely come to his shoulder. He could feel Emaline's breath on his cheek, warm and erratic. She was frightened, he realized. For a moment he considered lowering his lips to hers, punishing her with his mouth. But he didn't make war on women and children, and kissing her would be tantamount to an assault. He bore nothing but enmity for her and her people.

"Conn."

His body tensed at the raspy sound of his name on her lips. He looked down and felt a spiral of desire as she moistened her lips with her tongue. He had missed her mouth when he was cataloging her very few virtues. It was bowed on top, and the lower lip was full and enticing. It was a mouth made to be kissed.

But not by him.

He shoved her an arm's distance away. "This won't work," he said in a guttural voice. "What's to keep everyone from killing each other in spite of this arranged marriage?"

She looked up at him, and he found himself ensnared by her innocent blue eyes.

"Everyone will start sharing the water on the disputed land at once," Emaline explained. "Supposedly that's what we've been feuding over."

"You know that's not all there is to the feud," Conn insisted.

"Why else are we fighting?"

"For vengeance," Conn said. "To pay back —"

"Don't you see that has to end?" Emaline said. "The killing has to stop somewhere, sometime. Why not now? Why not with our marriage?"

"Confound it, woman, don't you see —"

"All I see is a stubborn man, intent on killing!"

"I lost my wife!"

"I lost my father and my brother! We've all lost family. What makes you different?"

Conn wanted to rant and rave, to cry out that he had loved with a passion beyond anything he had ever thought imaginable. That his life had ended when Josie died, and he had wished to go to the grave with her. That he didn't want to live without the only love he would ever know. That he didn't want to feel again, because pain was what he felt first and foremost.

"Say yes, Conn."

Her words were a plea, but there was nothing subservient in her posture. In fact, he would probably have to wrestle her to the ground to have any chance of bedding her. Except if she wanted the peace to last she would have to bear a child. His child. She would have to submit to him. Not someday, but on their wedding day, and every day after that until his seed began to grow inside her. The thought of touching her, of discovering whether her freckles truly covered every part of her body, heated his blood.

Guilt that he felt desire when he should be feeling hate made his voice harsh. "I want nothing to do with you outside of bed. I'll do what's necessary to make a

child with you, but that's all. Is that understood?"

He thought she winced, but if she did,
the expression was gone as quickly as it
had come, leaving only disdain for him.

"If that's the way you want it," she said.
"Are we agreed then?"

"I'll marry you," he agreed. "And God
help us both."

Two

The next time Conn and Emaline met was Saturday, the last day of the truce. They stood at the front of the Bitter Creek Baptist Church waiting for the preacher to speak the words that would bind them together for life. Anxious Winthrops sat to the left of the center aisle, nervous Bentons to the right. Conn's and Emaline's mothers exchanged concerned glances as they watched their respective children take their vows.

Emaline had made her own wedding dress. She had bought the pale peach silk with money she had earned selling eggs and butter. It had been lying folded in her cedar chest for three years. She couldn't have explained why she had spent the money for such a luxury, but when the traveling peddler had shown her the silk, she had known she had to have it. There had been no reason to make it into a dress until now.

Emaline hadn't realized until she had

slipped into the pale peach princess sheath this morning just how many dreams she had sewn into the garment. She knew Conn hated all Winthrops, but he was going to be her husband. She wanted him to be proud of her. She wanted him to admire her. She wanted to feel like a bride.

She had seen Conn's eyes widen in acknowledgement when he first spied her at the church, but he hadn't given her the compliments she yearned to hear. He had simply taken her hand in his and said, "Are you sure you want to go through with this?"

"I'm sure," she had replied.

"Then let's get it over with."

He had turned her to face the preacher, and the wedding ceremony had begun. Now Emaline felt a burning sensation in her nose that warned of tears. She swallowed hard and closed her eyes. She didn't want to be this man's wife. She was frightened of the night to come, when he would thrust himself inside her to plant his seed. Her mother had warned her it would hurt the first time, but only that one time. All Emaline could think of was the virulent hatred she had seen in Conn's eyes whenever he spoke of the Winthrops. She had always considered herself a courageous woman, but at the moment she was terrified.

Because he was holding Emaline Winthrop's hand, Conn felt her tremble as she spoke her vows. He wondered what was going on inside that pretty head of hers. And she was pretty, Conn admitted, damn near beautiful. The peach silk softened the effect of her freckles, and made her eyes look even bluer. Somehow she had managed to subdue her hair with a scant piece of netting and some paper flowers, though there were a few unruly curls around her temples and at her nape that made him want to touch her.

He should have told her she was beautiful. Every bride deserved to hear those words from her future husband on their wedding day. But the words had caught in his throat as a vision rose before him of Josie dressed all in white, her perfectly straight, dark brown hair confined securely at her nape, her bosom rising from the square neck of her linen and lace wedding gown, her hazel eyes alight with love for him. His wedding to Emaline Winthrop was merely a means to an end. Together they would stop the feud that had killed the woman he loved and so many, many others. She wasn't a real bride.

"If there is anyone present who knows any reason why these two should not be joined, let him speak now, or forever hold his peace."

The preacher's words dragged Conn from his ruminations. He waited with bated breath to hear an objection. Surely there would be one. Surely someone would put a stop to this insanity. But no one did.

The preacher had just begun to speak again when Devlin Winthrop leaped up from his seat in the front pew. "I have an objection," he said.

Every eye in the room focused on him. Emaline grabbed the skirt of her dress and swung it around to face her brother. "Please, Dev, don't."

"I have to, Emmy." Devlin turned his steady gaze on Conn. "I want a promise from you that you won't hurt my sister."

Emaline felt Conn stiffen beside her. His expression remained bland, but she sensed he was furious.

"I don't know a way to broach a virgin that doesn't hurt," Conn said in a quiet voice.

Several women gasped as they realized what Conn had said.

Emaline felt the damnable blush growing in her cheeks, but she refused to hide her face. It was no bad thing to be a virgin on one's wedding day.

"You know that's not what I mean," Devlin said, his own face flushed with anger and embarrassment.

"What *do* you mean?" Conn asked in a deadly voice.

"It's no secret my sister hates you and your kind."

Conn's face bleached white, but he said nothing as Devlin continued. "And you hate her, along with the rest of the Winthrops. I want your promise that you won't punish her for what others have done to you and yours. Otherwise, this wedding ends here."

Emaline had never been more proud of her brother. Or more frightened for him. Conn almost vibrated with animosity. She could feel the waves of tension rolling off him. Fortunately, all guns had been left outside the church. She let herself glance at Conn from the corner of her eye. The only outward evidence of his tremendous anger was a small muscle ticking in his cheek where his jaws must be clamped.

"You have my promise," he said from between clenched teeth. "Anything else?"

Emaline met Devlin's worried gaze. She knew he wanted to save her from her fate, but there was no help to be had. Someone had to marry Conn Benton.

Devlin searched Conn's dark eyes one last time, seeking reassurance. He must have found it because he said, "No. That's all."

"Well, then," the preacher said. "If that's settled, let us proceed."

Conn grasped Emaline's hand again, hard enough to hurt. With one look from her he loosened his grasp, but he didn't let go. Emaline had the feeling she had been claimed, and that Conn would kill the next man who tried to take her from him. It wasn't a bad feeling to have on one's wedding day.

Conn took a long, quiet breath and let it out as the preacher continued his incantations. He couldn't explain the rage he had felt when Emaline's brother challenged his right to marry her. But he wasn't sure whether he had been enraged at Devlin's suggestion that he would use his strength against a woman or whether he truly felt possessive of Emaline Winthrop. That seemed impossible, but the nagging feeling wouldn't leave him that she had given herself to him when she had put her hand in his at the beginning of the ceremony.

It wouldn't be long now before Emaline

was his wife. The preacher was getting to the vows Conn remembered from his first wedding. "Do you take this woman . . ."

Conn had trouble concentrating on the ceremony. He couldn't be pledging these things before God. *To love and to cherish?* Everyone present knew what a mockery that was. But when the preacher demanded an answer from him, he dutifully replied, "I do."

Emaline tried not to squirm when Conn said, "I do," but a trickle of sweat was stealing down between her breasts. It made a wonderful distraction as the preacher demanded her promise *to honor and obey* her husband. What a travesty! How could she honor any Benton much less obey him? But when the preacher asked for her response, she whispered an obedient "I do."

Before Emaline was ready, the preacher was saying, "I now pronounce you man and wife." There was a slight pause before he said, "You may kiss the bride, Mr. Benton."

Emaline felt breathless. Would he dare? She raised her eyes to meet Conn's dark-eyed gaze. What was expected of them? What would do the most to help ensure the peace? She saw the question in Conn's eyes.

Emaline nodded slightly. Her eyes fell closed as his mouth lowered. His lips were firm as he pressed them fleetingly against hers. She thought the kiss was over when his arms suddenly tightened around her, and his mouth claimed hers again.

There was nothing simple about the second kiss. It was full of anger and arrogance. And need. His tongue traced the seam of her lips, and when she gasped for air it slid inside. Emaline was totally unprepared for the sensations evoked by the warmth and wetness of his invasion.

Suddenly the kiss was over. When Emaline opened her eyes, Conn was staring out at the Benton side of the church with a smug grin on his face. All hail the conquering hero, it said.

Emaline had never felt more furious in her life. Or more humiliated. So Conn thought she could be dominated by a kiss, did he? Well, she would show him!

She kept her voice pitched low as she said, "Conn, darling?"

He was so shocked by the *darling* that he turned completely around to face her. She slipped her arms around his neck, pressed her body against his, and raised herself on tiptoes to reach his mouth. He was too surprised to protest as her lips pressed against his. Her mouth curved in a satisfied smile as she heard cheering from the Winthrop side of the church.

She should have known Conn wouldn't play fair.

Before she could retreat, he had his tongue in her mouth again. She gasped at the streak of excitement that ran from her belly upward as he grabbed her by the waist and brought their bodies together.

There was hooting now from both sides of the church and a few raucous hollers.

"Give up?" Conn murmured against her lips.

"Never!" Emaline replied.

Their mothers came to the rescue.

"Conn, dear, please let me welcome my new daughter," Hester said.

"And I want to meet my new son," said Emaline's mother, Clara. It was easy to see where Emaline and Devlin had gotten their height and features. Clara Winthrop was barely an inch shorter than her son, yet she possessed a certain grace that kept her from seeming as tall as she was. She had the same auburn hair as Devlin and Emaline's blue eyes.

The two combatants were forced to disengage. Emaline turned to Mrs. Benton. Conn turned to Mrs. Winthrop. Each hugged their respective mothers-in-law. Then they turned and marched down the aisle together as the organ played a triumphant tune.

A reception was held for the bride and groom at the home of Archer Tubbston, the town banker. Besides the two families, several interested townspeople — merchants and such — had also attended the wedding, sitting in the very back pews. Archer Tubbston was among them. When he had heard about the wedding, he had insisted on hosting the reception. "After all," he had said, "it isn't every day a feud ends."

Emaline didn't see why Mr. Tubbston was so glad to see the feud ended. The bank had made a fortune foreclosing on properties when a rancher was killed and the surviving widow couldn't meet the mortgage payments. But she supposed everyone would be glad to know the streets were safe to walk again. There had been some incidents over the years in which innocent people — neither Bentons nor Winthrops — had been hurt. The cattle stampede through Bitter Creek that had killed Rufus Winthrop, Sissy Benton, and Bethanne Fleet was just one example.

Neither Bentons nor Winthrops would

admit to firing the first shot that had started the stampede. It had simply been a case of one of the numerous altercations between warring factions getting out of hand. Clearly, both sides were to blame. The senseless feud had caused three senseless deaths. No wonder Bethanne's father was inconsolable, Emaline thought.

The punch at the reception was nonalcoholic, and though there were musicians, there was no dancing. At least, not at first. One of the differences between Winthrops and Bentons was how strictly they followed Baptist tenets. Winthrops drank but didn't dance. Bentons danced but didn't drink.

Emaline should have suspected that Conn would ask his bride to dance. As soon as the violins began to play a waltz, he turned to her and said, "Shall we dance?"

She was sure he expected her to refuse, thereby creating a confrontation. She was equally determined to avoid an altercation at all costs. The solution was obvious. She simply said, "I don't know how."

"It's easy. I'll teach you," Conn replied.

He didn't offer her a choice in the matter. Emaline tensed as Conn's hand slid around her waist. It appeared there was no avoiding the situation. She laid her hand in his palm and allowed him to move her in time to the music.

"Just count one-two-three, one-two-three," Conn instructed as he swung her in ever-widening circles around the Tubbston's parlor.

Emaline felt as if she were flying. She had never realized how much fun it was to dance, otherwise she would surely have sinned much sooner. She ignored her brother's glare as she whirled by him. It was past time the Winthrops learned to be a bit more tolerant of the Bentons. Dancing was perfectly harmless.

Then she realized that Conn had closed the space between them until no more than an inch separated them. She felt his breath against her cheek, felt the heat of him along the entire length of her body, which was responding in strange and wonderful ways. No wonder the preacher had called dancing "a fornication of the spirit." She had never been so aware of a man as she was of Conn. It was like making love standing up fully clothed in a roomful of people!

When the dance ended, Emaline tore herself free and walked quickly toward an empty corner of the room. Conn followed her.

"What's wrong?" he asked.

"Nothing. I've never danced before, that's all. I had no idea . . ."

"It could be so much fun?" Conn finished.

"It could feel so sinful!" Emaline snapped back.

"Could feel so sinfully good, you mean."

"Everything we do together from now on will be subject to scrutiny," Emaline said, keeping her voice low. "I would simply prefer not to give my friends and family any more reason to talk about us than they already have."

"I see."

Conn wondered, not for the first time, what it would be like to have Emaline Winthrop beneath him in bed. He had been surprised by her willingness to dance, pleased by how quickly she had caught the rhythm of the waltz, and appalled by how much he had wanted to feel her body moving in concert with his.

He had loved dancing with Josie, but the differences in their heights had made it more difficult to stay in step. Emaline had moved with him as though they had been dancing together for years. It had been an unsettling experience, but one that he realized he was more than willing to repeat.

But perhaps Emaline was right. There was no sense making a spectacle of themselves.

"All right. If you don't want to dance, perhaps we should find somewhere to sit and have something to eat."

Conn took Emaline's elbow to lead her toward the immense tables of food that had been set out. It was then he noticed Devlin Winthrop dancing . . . with Conn's own widowed sister-in-law.

Conn stopped dead in his tracks, his hold on Emaline's arm necessarily bringing her to a halt as well. She looked up at him, then followed the direction of his gaze to the dance floor. She couldn't have been more shocked. Her brother, Devlin, was dancing! She hadn't even suspected he knew how. Even more shocking was the fact he was dancing with a Benton woman.

Emaline was immediately aware of the hush that had fallen in the Tubbstons' parlor. It was all well and good for Emaline and Conn to dance. They were setting an example for the future. But it seemed the future was collapsing in on them. Emaline wondered what had possessed Devlin to approach the woman. And why she had accepted his offer to dance.

Because Emaline was watching the couple closely, she saw something that made her blood run cold. She recognized the look on the woman's face, because she had experienced the same feeling with Conn. Carnal awareness arced between her brother and the Benton woman. They never took their eyes off each other, and their bodies seemed to hum with sensual energy.

Because she was just learning to recognize the signs herself, it took Emaline a moment to realize that Conn saw the same thing she did. Before she could stop him, he stalked past her, headed for the dance floor. Emaline hurried to catch up with him.

She used those few moments to take the Benton woman's measure. She was petite, with dark brown hair and brown eyes. She was also slender, but with the full bosom and hips that Emaline lacked. Devlin's head was bent over to listen as the woman spoke to him. There was a smile on her brother's lips.

Fortunately, the dance was just ending, so as far as the rest of the guests were concerned, it appeared that Conn and Emaline were merely greeting the other couple.

Before Conn could say a word, Emaline slipped her arm through his and said, "I didn't know you two were acquainted." Emaline faced the Benton woman. "We haven't met. I'm Emaline Win — Benton," she finished.

"I'm Melody Benton."

"My brother Andrew's widow," Conn supplied in a steely voice. He fixed a glare on Devlin. "I'm warning you now to stay away from my sister-in-law."

"Melody might have something to say about that," Devlin replied.

"She doesn't know Winthrops like I do," Conn said.

"Meaning what?" Devlin challenged.

"Please, Dev," Melody said in a quiet voice, laying her hand on Devlin's sleeve. "Remember your promise."

The fact that Melody had used Devlin's nickname gave Emaline pause. She stared entranced as her brother laid a gentle hand over Melody's. Promise? What promise? Hadn't the two of them just met? Obviously not. But when had their romance begun, and how? Emaline wanted to get Devlin alone to question him.

"All right, Melody. I won't cause any trouble," Devlin said. He turned to Conn. "I don't want to fight with you."

"Then let go of my brother's wife."

Conn had given his order in a voice that

could be heard around the room. Emaline saw the subtle shifting as Winthrops and Bentons aligned themselves on opposite sides. The truce was in danger of exploding into violence right here and now. If she'd had a skillet handy she would have used it on Conn. How could he endanger the truce now!

Emaline saw the way Devlin's fist clenched, saw Melody's face turn white, and knew she had to find a way to stop this altercation before it got started. Melody beat her to it.

"Andrew is dead, Conn. He has been for five years. I'm a grown woman. I can take care of myself."

"As guardian of my brother's children, I think I have some say —"

"You have nothing to say in this," Devlin interrupted.

"The hell I don't!"

"Dev! Conn!" Emaline put herself physically between the two men. "In case you've both forgotten, this is my wedding day. I won't have my husband and my brother coming to blows. Is that understood?" She fixed each of them with a warning glare.

Emaline noticed the way Melody's hand tightened on Devlin's arm. Her own hand tightened on Conn's sleeve. At that moment the musicians began to play another waltz.

Emaline turned to face her husband. "Shall we dance, Conn?"

Conn hesitated a moment, until Devlin led Melody off the dance floor, then he swept Emaline into his arms.

Emaline felt a palpable easing of tension in the parlor. Bentons and Winthrops mingled again and began to talk in low tones. The danger had passed.

Emaline recognized Conn's anger in the tautness of his shoulder where her hand rested. It was better, she believed, to confront the problem than to ignore it so she said, "How long do you think they've known each other?"

Conn let out a gusty sigh. "Hell if I know. But it's plain as a red barn they didn't just meet today."

"I always wondered why Dev never married," Emaline murmured. "Now I understand. How awful it must have been for them, to be in love yet not free to be together."

"Oh, they've been together. I'd lay odds on that," Conn said with a snarl of disgust.

Emaline realized suddenly the cause of all Dev's spluttering when she had first suggested a Winthrop marry a Benton. He must have wanted to shout that he and Melody would be a better couple to marry under the circumstances. Obviously, it would have been difficult to suggest such a thing when he supposedly didn't even know her. Nor could he speak for Melody without having a chance to ask her whether it was what she wanted. And things had been settled on the spot.

Emaline felt a sharp pang of regret. Her wedding to Conn might not have been necessary. On the other hand, she could see a multitude of problems that would have arisen if Dev and Melody had admitted to their clandestine relationship. Accusations and admonitions such as the ones Conn had hurled might have been made on both sides. It was better this way, she concluded. Besides, it was too late to change anything now. She was already married to Conn.

"To have to meet in secret can't have been what either of them wanted," Emaline said, raising her eyes to meet Conn's. "If I were in love —"

She cut herself off. Love wasn't any part of her arrangement with Conn Benton. Nor did it seem he had any sympathy for her brother and his sister-in-law. His hate and distrust of Bentons had been growing for years. Saying words before a preacher hadn't done a thing to ease his animosity. Emaline bit her lip to hold back the cry of despair that sought voice. She had embarked on a fool's errand. She would be lucky if she survived it whole.

Someone had secretly added liquor to the punch, and the reception gradually became rowdy. There were minor fracases, which either Jeremiah or Horace managed to quell.

Emaline looked for John Fleet at the reception, but couldn't find him. She took advantage of a moment when Conn was involved in drinking toasts with his friends and family to escape the noise and commotion. She was subjected to a few stares from passersby, which she ignored as she made her way down Main Street, but she didn't return to the reception. She needed to be alone for a little while.

Emaline hadn't realized herself where she was going until she found herself at the door to the blacksmith's shop. Fleet shouldn't have been there, since it was nearly dusk. To her surprise, he was working at the forge. Sweat glistened on his hairy torso, which was bare except for a worn leather apron. A red bandanna caught the rivulets of perspiration that ran down his neck.

Without a thought to what damage the pervasive soot or an errant spark could do to her wedding dress, she entered the darkened interior of the shop. She stared, fascinated, as the bellows heated the embers. A horseshoe lay in the fire, turning a glowing red from the heat. Fleet held the shoe with a set of tongs, and as she watched he withdrew it from the fire and shaped it with deafening blows from a heavy hammer.

She wasn't sure how long she had been standing there when he finally noticed her. He wasn't happy to see her.

"What do you want now?" he demanded.

Emaline swallowed hard. "I suppose you know I married Conn Benton today."

"Yeah. So what?"

"The feud is over now," Emaline said. "Or it will be soon," she hurried to amend. A baby had to be born first.

"Am I supposed to be happy about that?"

"Well, yes," Emaline said. "It will mean an end to the killing."

He looked at her with sad eyes and spoke in a bitter voice. "It comes too late. My daughter is dead."

He plunged the horseshoe back into the fire and ignored her as though she wasn't even there. Emaline backed out of the shop and ran down the back alleys until she reached the Tubbstons' house, breathless and trembling. She merged with the crowd that had spread out through the back door as though she had never been gone.

It wasn't for nothing, she thought. *It may be too late for Bethanne, but not for a lot of others.*

Emaline was still a little breathless, though her trembling had stopped, when it was time for the bride and groom to head for home. Conn lifted her into a spring wagon he had brought to take her to his ranch. Sometime during the reception, the wagon had been decorated with ribbons and paper bunting. Everyone followed in wagons and carriages and on horseback. They all had an interest in making sure this marriage was consummated.

Meanwhile Emaline's virginal fears grew to monstrous proportions. It was bad enough to be facing a stranger in bed. It was a hundred times worse knowing he cared little or nothing for her feelings. This was not what she had envisioned when she thought of her wedding night. Emaline suddenly wasn't sure she could go through with it.

It was nearly dark by the time they arrived at Conn's ranch house. It was a one-story dogtrot home common to this part of Texas, with a central hallway running down the middle and rooms on either side. Emaline noticed the wood-frame structure had a fresh coat of white paint.

Conn's hands were warm through her dress as he lifted her down from the wagon seat. She was horribly aware of the blush on her face as he hefted her into his arms — what a feat that would have been for most men! — and carried her over the threshold of his home.

He kicked the door closed behind them before setting her back on her feet. She was aware of the raucous catcalls and lascivious jeers just beyond the door. Tears welled in her eyes, and she wasn't sure what to do about them. One spilled before she could blink it back.

"Well," Conn said.

That was all. Not, *Welcome to my home.* Just, *Well.*

Emaline couldn't blame him. She felt overwhelmed herself. How had they let themselves get talked into this?

"What shall we do now?" Conn said at last.

Emaline couldn't look at him. "I don't know."

"We have to —"

"Please," Emaline interrupted. "I know what I've agreed to do. Can't we wait? Just a little while?"

"It'll only get harder," Conn said.

"I can't do it," Emaline said quietly. "Not like this. I don't even know you."

"Fine," Conn said, his voice no less quiet or agitated than hers. "I'll go out there and tell them we've changed our minds."

He had his hand on the doorknob when Emaline spoke.

"All right. You win."

He turned a bleak look on her. "No, Emaline," he said, using her name for the first time, "I think we've both lost."

They stood frozen in a tableau of tragedy, of love lost and love uncelebrated. Until at last Conn reached out a hand toward her. "Let's go to bed, Emaline."

She took the two steps necessary to place her palm in his and looked up at him with somber eyes. "Please be gentle, Conn."

His hand clasped hers and gently squeezed. "I'll do my best."

Conn led Emaline to his bedroom door

and left her there. "I'll be back in a little while," he said.

Emaline closed the door. It was already dusk, and there was barely enough light to see what she was doing. She noted the large four-poster bed and found the dry sink with a pitcher and bowl and a wardrobe where Conn must keep his clothing. There was also a long low cedar chest — his former wife's hope chest? — at the foot of the bed. She could feel the rag rug beneath her feet and see a slight shine on the hardwood floors in the rest of the room.

Emaline was afraid to light a lamp, knowing the wild crowd outside would realize where she was and hoot and howl all the louder. So she undressed in the dark, letting her precious wedding dress drop to the floor at her feet and then stepping out of it. It didn't take long to strip down to her chemise and pantalets. She had delivered a carpetbag of clothing to Conn's house the previous day, and it was beside the chest at the foot of the bed.

She opened it and quickly pulled out a chambray wrapper that would cover her from neck to ankles. She debated whether to leave on her chemise and pantalets, but decided it was better to take them off. If Conn planned to undress her, she didn't want to prolong the agony. She stripped down and slid the nightgown over her head. It was an old garment, and the fabric had been worn soft and smooth.

Emaline turned back the covers and slid underneath them. She sat upright, her back braced against the pillow at the head of the bed, and waited for Conn to appear.

He was nothing more than a shadow when he entered the room, it was so dark, but she could see enough to know he was wearing only his long johns. He quickly slipped under the covers to lie beside her.

"You could have lit a candle," he said.

"You know why I didn't," she retorted. "Some of the ribald things they're yelling aren't fit —" Emaline cut herself off. There was no sense angering him, especially not now.

The noise from outside of a shivaree in full swing — a serenade in pots and pans to the newly married couple by both their families — was the only sound in the silent room.

At last Conn sighed. "Emaline, I don't know a way . . ." He paused and started again. "I have to . . ."

"I know," she said. He had made his feelings clear at church. There was no way he knew to prevent a virgin's pain. Emaline inched down until she was lying flat in the bed. "Just get it over with, Conn. Please."

Conn didn't feel in the least aroused. It had occurred to him once before that he might not be able to perform on cue, but he figured things weren't going to get any better if he laid here thinking about it. So he reached over and grabbed a handful of her gown and began to move it out of his way.

He could feel Emaline's rigidity as he said, "Lift your hips." She moved so he could shove the nightgown up. He felt himself becoming aroused as his hand brushed the softness of her skin. It seemed his curiosity about her freckles wasn't going to be assuaged, at least not tonight. The room was pitch black. He was feeling his way through what had to be done.

He eased himself onto her, bracing most of his weight on his elbows. "Spread your legs, Emaline," he murmured against her cheek. Conn realized his body was ready, even if his mind still shied from what was before him. At least he would be able to finish without entirely losing his dignity.

Emaline blessed the darkness that hid her fear and embarrassment. She grasped Conn's shoulders. "Conn. Please." She wouldn't beg him not to hurt her. She had too much pride for that. But it was frightening to be so vulnerable to him. She shivered as his hand slid down her belly. "Conn?"

"Lie still, Emaline. I just want to see . . ." His voice drifted away as his hand slid between her thighs.

Emaline pressed her legs tightly together. "What are you doing?" she demanded.

"Emaline," he said patiently, "I'm doing what a husband does with his wife."

"Oh." She forced herself to relax, allowed her legs to ease open enough to allow Conn's hand free access.

She gasped as he cupped her, then slowly parted the folds and tried to slide a finger inside her.

"That hurts, Conn," she said in a ragged voice.

His finger withdrew. "You're as dry as a bone," he said in disgust.

Emaline lay still. "Is that bad?"

"Bad enough," he admitted.

"I . . ." She swallowed over the painful lump in her throat. "Is there something I should do?"

Conn had two choices. He could take her now and get it over with, or he could spend some time arousing her first. He wanted this over with, but it was going to be hard enough for her without making it any worse.

"There are things I can do, Emaline, to make this easier."

"Such as?" she ventured cautiously.

"Your body isn't ready for mine. I have to . . . to touch you."

"Oh."

"I can do what's necessary to help your body accommodate mine better. Or I can just get it over with right now," Conn said. "The choice is yours."

Emaline thought about it a moment. "If there's a way to make it easier . . . I'd rather you do that."

"Let's get rid of this nightgown, shall we?" Conn said.

He was already tugging it up over her head as he spoke, not really giving Emaline the option to refuse. A moment later she was naked. She had sat up as he tugged off the gown, and Conn pressed her shoulder to lower her back to the pillow. It took her a few moments to realize he was stripping himself, as well. Lord, she was grateful for the dark!

"Relax, Emaline," he instructed. "I'll do all the work."

Since she had never planned to marry,

she had never been courted. Not that she hadn't been kissed when she was younger, thirteen or fourteen. But those kisses had been nothing like the kisses Conn placed on her body now. And she was totally unprepared for the feelings Conn aroused as his callused fingertips caressed her. She was soon writhing beneath him. "Conn," she said desperately, "what are you doing? I feel . . . I can't . . ."

Conn told himself he was only doing as much as was necessary to prevent hurting his wife any more than he had to when he broached her. But she was so responsive! Her back arched as his hands cupped her breasts — a bare handful. And she groaned, a wrenching guttural sound, as his lips closed on a nipple. He suckled and her hips rose to search out his own.

He didn't kiss her on the mouth. That would have made more of this than it truly was. He had a job to do, that was all. He wasn't making love to her, he was merely coupling with her.

Nevertheless, he couldn't resist touching her. Her skin was so incredibly soft. He tried to imagine the sight of her freckles beneath his fingertips, but couldn't. His hand slid down her hip, across a flat stomach and into a nest of curls, which he suddenly realized must be as red as her hair.

That was better. She was wet now. He could do what had to be done.

But he wasn't willing yet to stop touching her. She couldn't know that what he did now wasn't strictly necessary. He indulged his need to feel her flesh beneath his fingertips. His hand slid up to grip her waist, then followed the outline of her slender hip back down her thigh all the way to her knee. Then he caressed his way back up the inside of her leg to the folds that he parted for a more intimate invasion. He heard Emaline catch her breath as his finger intruded. But the way was slick now, and his finger slid easily inside.

Until he reached the proof of her virginity.

It reminded him of what he was supposed to do. Broach her. Get her with child.

It was time to get on with business.

Emaline had never felt more strange. She was in a euphoric state that made time stand still. She knew it couldn't be long now. She had recognized the difference when Conn touched her. "Conn?" she questioned.

"Lie still, Emaline. I'll try not to hurt

you any more than I have to."

She braced her hands on his arms. The muscles were hard, and she realized suddenly how strong he must be. She could not stop him, not if he didn't want to be stopped. She was totally at his mercy.

Conn pushed her legs farther apart with his knees. His body was slick with a sheen of sweat. He wanted her. His body ached with wanting. It had been a long time, and his heart pounded. He tried to go slow, to enter her a little at a time, but he felt her tensing and realized the longer she had to anticipate the moment the worse it was going to be.

He thrust hard and felt the membrane give way at the same instant that she gave a sharp cry of pain.

He held himself perfectly still. "It's done now, Emaline. The painful part is over."

There was a moment of silence before she said in a small voice, "But you're not finished, are you?"

He felt his smile and was glad she couldn't see it. "No. I'm not finished yet. There is the seed to plant."

"Oh."

He began to move slightly, feeling the exquisite friction of their bodies as he lifted himself away from her and then thrust again. He felt her lift her hips to meet him and almost groaned aloud. It was a matter of embarrassingly few moments before he spilled his seed.

He rolled away, releasing his hold on her. He lay on his back with an arm across his eyes. His breathing was ragged. It had felt good. Too good. He wanted her again already, and he knew that was impossible.

The last thing he heard before he fell asleep was the sound of his new wife sobbing quietly against her pillow.

Three

Emaline was crying with relief and regret, but there was no way she could have told Conn that, even if he had asked. Which he didn't. The reason for her relief was obvious. The ordeal she had so feared was over. She had managed to survive their first coupling, and though it had hurt, she sensed the pain wasn't as bad as it would have been if Conn hadn't taken the time to prepare her first. She would always be grateful to him for that kindness.

It was the regret that kept her awake long past the time when Conn's steady breathing told her he was asleep. She was glad he had fallen asleep so quickly, leaving her alone to contemplate the past few hours of her life. Only, her thoughts were so confused that perhaps it would have been better if she wasn't doing any thinking. Because all she could imagine was what might have been. If there had been no feud. If a handsome beau had courted her. If she had married a man who loved her.

She heard the shivaree winding down until at last all the revelers were gone. She must have fallen asleep, for she woke as the first rays of dawn lightened the room.

It seemed strange to have someone else in bed with her. She was alarmed at first because she and Conn were lying nose to nose, their foreheads nearly touching. She gradually inched her way back until she could observe him sleeping. His face had a stubble of dark beard, and she noticed for the first time how long and full his lashes were against his cheeks. There was a tiny scar that cut through one eyebrow, and she could see a faint tan line where his Stetson kept the sun off his forehead.

His hair looked silky. When she reached out slowly, carefully, to touch it, he awoke. She jerked her hand back and lowered her lids so he couldn't see her eyes.

"Good morning," he said in a sleep-husky voice. "Did you sleep well?"

"Well enough," she said in a more than normally raspy voice. She was watching Conn, so she saw the moment when he remembered who she was, and who he was.

Enemies in bed together. Enemies forced to pretend that everything was normal. Enemies forced to spend their lives together.

The amiability in his voice was gone when he asked, "What are the chances of getting some breakfast?"

Breakfast? They were lying naked in bed together, and his mind was on breakfast? She would have grinned if the situation wasn't so dire. Emaline had often chided her brother for thinking often and only of his stomach, but it appeared it was a trait common to the male sex. "I'll be glad to fix you something. That is, if you'll give me a moment to dress."

Emaline waited for him to realize she wanted him to leave the room. He was a perceptive man. What she didn't count on was that he would have no modesty himself. He simply shoved the covers aside and stood, completely naked, and stretched.

She knew she shouldn't look, but once she glanced toward Conn, she couldn't take her eyes off him. In the daylight he was a magnificent creature of bone and sinew, tall and lean without an ounce of extra flesh. The languid stretch reminded her of a sleek cat, supremely confident and at ease. He crossed to the wardrobe and drew out another set of long johns, which he quickly donned. Minutes later he was completely dressed, right down to his boots.

"I'll go light a fire in the stove and put on the coffeepot," he said. "I usually shave after breakfast, unless that's a problem for you."

"No problem." Emaline wouldn't have said she minded even if she did. She wasn't about to ask any favors of Conn. Once he was gone, she scrambled out of bed and hurried over to the pitcher she had noted last night on the dry sink to see if there was water to wash herself. There was, and she quickly finished her ablutions and dressed in another outfit from her carpetbag. The rest of her belongings were to be delivered to Conn's ranch today.

Emaline took one look at the smear of blood on the sheets and quickly stripped them. She usually did laundry on Monday, but unless Conn had extra sheets, she was going to have to do the washing today.

Conn was amazed at how soon Emaline appeared in the bedroom doorway dressed in a calico skirt and a long-sleeved cotton shirtwaist that buttoned all the way up to the round-necked collar. There was nothing the least bit enticing about what she was wearing, yet his heart thumped once when he laid eyes on her, and his groin tightened at the pleasurable memory of what it felt like to be inside her. It wasn't going to be as easy to ignore his new wife as he had hoped.

Emaline took a deep breath. "The coffee smells good." She stood in the small kitchen and realized she didn't know where anything was. And she had promised to make breakfast. She wasn't sure whether to start rummaging through cupboards or simply join him at the table.

Thankfully, Conn seemed to realize her problem. He stood and began rummaging through the cupboards himself. "Pots and pans are stored here," he said, pulling out a skillet and dropping it on top of the stove. "Dishes and silverware are in the sideboard. Cups are hung there, too. Eggs are in the wire basket in the icebox, along with the milk. Bacon hangs in the pantry along with preserves and canned goods and such like."

Conn had been collecting items as he showed her where they were, so that soon Emaline had everything she needed to make eggs and bacon. "If you want biscuits, you're going to have to show me where to find flour, salt, lard and baking soda," she said.

"Don't have time to wait for anything to bake this morning," he said. "Have to get started right away on some fence mending. Just eggs and bacon will be fine."

Emaline became increasingly flustered as Conn watched her with an intent stare while she worked. "How do you like your eggs?" she asked as she cut strips of bacon and laid them in the skillet.

"Fried with the yellow soft," he said. "And I like my bacon crisp."

Emaline must have cooked a thousand eggs in her life, but this morning she managed to break the yolks. The three eggs were as hard as shoe leather by the time she set them in front of Conn. Worse, in her attempt to get the bacon crisp, she had burned it nearly black. She knew nothing about her husband, whether he had a temper, whether he was tolerant, whether he could become violent. It was with some trepidation that she set the plate in front of him.

"I'm sorry, Conn. I'm a good cook. I don't know what went wrong this morning."

She expected him to gripe, but to her surprise he simply ate the hardened eggs and the blackened bacon.

"I expect you'll get better," he said through a mouthful of food.

Emaline wasn't sure whether his comment was intended as encouragement or warning.

"Actually, this breakfast reminds me of the first meal Josie made for me. We were so busy kissing that she forgot all about —" Conn cut himself off.

Emaline's face paled. So that was her name . . . Josie. The last thing she wanted was for Conn to compare her to his dead wife. She especially didn't want to be reminded how much in love with her he had been. Conn must have realized his mistake, because he didn't say another word until he had finished eating.

"I've got some chores to do in the barn before I leave. I'll eat chow with the hands at noon and be back around sundown. Make yourself to home."

"You haven't shaved," she reminded him.

"Sometimes I don't," he admitted as he closed the kitchen door behind him and headed for the barn.

He didn't kiss her as he left for the day. He didn't even look at her.

Emaline sat frozen in her chair at the trestle table that dominated the kitchen. Everywhere she turned there were reminders of Conn's first wife. The lace-edged yellow curtains in the kitchen window. Flowers embroidered on a sampler that had been framed and hung on the

233

wall. The homemade rag rug in front of the sink. The vase in the center of the table that must have once held flowers. The tiger-coated cat that sat patiently by a bowl in the corner, waiting for it to be filled with leftover milk from breakfast.

Emaline jumped up and ran into the parlor. It held a piano covered with a lacy doily and two carved wooden candlesticks with the candles half burned down. The horsehair sofa was barely worn, but doilies covered the arms. She searched the room and found what she was looking for: a brass-framed daguerreotype of the loving couple on the mantel above the brick fireplace.

Conn looked so young! As she had suspected, Josie was more than pretty: she was beautiful. There wasn't a wayward curl or a freckle on her. Emaline set the photograph back where she had found it and hurried to the bedroom she had shared with Conn the previous night. She yanked up the lid of the chest at the foot of the bed and gave a cry of despair.

It was filled with baby clothes.

Emaline sank to the floor beside the chest. Conn hadn't just loved Josie, they were apparently planning to have a child together when her life was cut short.

How awful it must be for Conn, how awful it was for both of them, to be trying to have a child now, not because they wanted one, but to end a years'-long feud.

Emaline reached into the chest and took out one of the cotton sacques Josie Benton had sewn. It was so tiny! She pulled out a small crocheted cap and booties. Another sacque. And diapers, dozens of diapers. At the bottom she found a linen and lace dress. It had to be Josie's wedding dress. She dropped it as though it had burned her.

Emaline laid her head on her arms on the edge of the chest and wept. It was all well and good to decide upon a noble sacrifice, but the reality of the situation was daunting. She tried to imagine what her future with Conn would be like, but the picture was grim.

It wasn't just that they were enemies. She assumed that with time they would become familiar with each other, and the strain she had felt this morning would eventually dissipate. She hadn't let herself consider what it would be like if they never became more than strangers. Although she couldn't imagine how they could remain strangers with the intimacy they were forced to endure.

Emaline tried not to resent the evidence of another woman in this house. But she was only human. This was *her* home now. Yet the ghost of Josie Benton, a woman her husband had obviously loved, still resided here. Not that she wanted Conn to love her. She didn't care if he hated her until the day she died. But she refused to live the rest of her life in another woman's shadow.

Emaline's head rose from her hands until her chin was angled pugnaciously. Conn had told her to make herself at home. Well, that was just what she would do! That meant putting her own imprint on the house. And removing every trace of Josie Benton.

Conn spent most of the morning distracted by memories of the night just past. He remembered how vehemently he had fought against marriage to a Winthrop. He remembered how shocked he had been at Emaline's height and appearance the day he met her. And he remembered making love to her last night.

He tried not to compare it to his wedding night with Josie, but that was impossible. It was painful to admit that he had been a better husband to Emaline than to

Josie. Of course, the years he'd spent with Josie had taught him how to treat a woman in bed. But it was more than that. Quite simply, the two women were different.

He had never thought much about it, but he had expected Emaline to be just like Josie, to act and react like her. But she wasn't Josie, and her responses had made him respond differently to her. His sister-in-law, Melody, had explained a similar phenomenon to him with regard to her two sons.

When Timmy had come along, she had expected him to be just like James. But the two boys were completely different, she had said, one sleeping through the night, the other up at odd hours. One liked peas, the other didn't. One had hazel eyes, the other brown. It didn't make one more lovable than the other. It just made them different.

That was what he had discovered with Emaline. She wasn't Josie. She was a separate person, with feelings and hopes and dreams that were nothing like his first wife's. Emaline was not more or less lovable. Just different.

By mid-morning Emaline had gathered up every bit of evidence that another woman had ever occupied the house and had piled it on the kitchen table. She opened the door to the stove, prepared to throw in the embroidered sampler that had adorned the kitchen wall.

But she couldn't do it.

She stared at the flames, wondering what on Earth had come over her. Even if she burned everything in the house, it wasn't going to erase the memories of Josie Benton that Conn carried in his mind and heart. And why was she so anxious to have Conn forget Josie, anyway? Theirs was strictly a marriage of convenience. Nothing more was necessary than that they tolerate each other long enough to produce a child.

Emaline wanted more than that. She wanted her husband to like her. Oh, fiddle. She wanted her husband to love her. Only, she had this slight problem. Conn was a Benton. And Bentons had always hated Winthrops.

But the feud was over. Or would be as soon as she birthed a child to inherit the disputed land. If the peace was to continue, it was necessary for everyone to forgive and forget past transgressions. She had lived her whole life hating Bentons, but that had to cease. Why not begin her forgiveness with Conn?

Conn was the man who would be the father of her children. He was the man who would take her to his bed for all the years to come. She found it impossible to face the thought of how lonely her life would be if she and Conn never learned to care for each other.

And she wasn't going to win Conn's heart by destroying everything that had to do with Josie. She would have to find another way to supplant the memories of his first wife. But she had no idea how a woman made a man fall in love with her. Especially when it was necessary for him to stop hating her first.

Emaline carefully replaced everything she had removed, including the tiny, delicate sacques and the christening gown she had found in the cedar chest at the foot of the four-poster.

By the time Devlin arrived with her things, she was in the middle of scrubbing floors and washing sheets. She was perfectly willing to stop what she was doing to ask Devlin about his relationship with Melody Benton, but Devlin refused to be interrogated.

"Let it be, Emmy," he said. "Melody and I have to work things out for ourselves. More importantly, how are you doing?"

Emaline had difficulty meeting his eyes. "I'm fine, Dev."

"He didn't hurt you?"

Emaline felt the heat begin at her throat and head toward her cheeks. "No," she said in a whisper.

Devlin put a hand on her chin and tipped it up so she was forced to meet his gaze. "Don't lie to me, Emmy."

"I'm not lying, Dev. I'm fine."

He seemed satisfied with what he saw and let her go. "Do you want help unloading the wagon?"

"I'm not ready to bring anything into the house just yet," she said. "I can handle it myself later."

"I'll be leaving then," Devlin said. "I'll be back to pick up the wagon later." He untied the horse that was hitched to the back of the wagon and mounted. "Take care of yourself, Emmy."

Emaline put a hand across her brow to shade her eyes from the sun as she looked up at her brother. "Maybe you can bring Melody to supper sometime."

"Maybe," Devlin said. "We'll see."

Emaline spent the rest of the day cleaning house and rearranging things, not removing signs of Josie, but adding tokens of her own. Conn had kept his house neat, but she wondered how long it had been since someone had taken a mop to the floors or a dustrag to the furniture. She felt a tremendous sense of satisfaction when she was done.

Conn was mending fence when he heard someone approaching on horseback. He put down his fence pliers and picked up his Winchester even as he turned to meet whoever had come calling. The truce wasn't old enough yet to set aside caution.

"Howdy," Devlin said as he halted his horse ten feet from the bore of the rifle Conn had pointed at him.

"I thought we finished our business yesterday," Conn said.

Devlin took his time dismounting, careful to keep his hands in plain sight at all times. "I just left a wagon at your place piled high with the rest of Emmy's things. I would have stayed to help her unload them, but she said she has some cleaning to do first."

"So why are you here?"

"I've got something to discuss with you."

"I'm not interested in anything you have to say, Winthrop."

"I want to marry Melody. As her closest male relative —"

"No."

"Melody and I love each other."

"No."

"We've loved each other for three years."

Conn's lips flattened and a muscle in his jaw worked. "Been sneaking around behind my back to see her?"

Devlin flushed, but there was nothing apologetic in his expression. "We couldn't be seen together without causing trouble. It seemed safer for everyone to be discreet. It hasn't been easy to love each other, but we do."

"The answer is still no."

"You can't stop us," Devlin said in a voice that was all the more threatening because of its quiet firmness.

"I can take Melody's boys from her if she marries you," Conn threatened.

Devlin's face paled. "She loves James and Timmy more than life. It would kill her to lose her sons."

"Then leave her alone."

"You're being unreasonable," Devlin said, his temper beginning to slip. "Why is it wrong for me and Melody to marry? There's an open-ended truce between Bentons and Winthrops now. The feud is over."

"*Maybe* it's over," Conn corrected.

"What's that supposed to mean?"

"It means I don't trust a Winthrop any farther than I can throw one," Conn replied. "It means this truce may last forever, or it may be over tomorrow if some Winthrop breaks the peace."

"Nobody's that stupid," Devlin said. "We're sharing the water now. There's no reason to fight anymore."

As he finished speaking, gunshots rang out.

"I knew it wouldn't last," Conn muttered.

"Those came from the creek," Devlin said.

Both men raced for their horses and galloped them in the direction of the gunshots. They arrived in time to see Winthrops and Bentons lined up on opposite sides of Bitter Creek with their guns drawn, while cattle milled about in the water.

"What's going on here?" Conn demanded.

"Someone took a shot at me from up in those trees," Eustis Benton said, pointing across the creek to a spot behind the Winthrops.

"If a Winthrop was shootin' at you,

you'd be dead!" Slim Winthrop retorted. His gun was still in his holster, but there were three Winthrops behind him with rifles in their hands. "Seemed to me that shot was meant to gun *me* down," Slim said.

"Bentons ain't in the habit of shootin' people in the back," Eustis said.

"No telling what a lily-livered, low-down skunk of a Benton would do," Slim replied.

Conn could see what was coming. The name calling would escalate until blood was shed. He gave an inward sigh of disgust. He wasn't going to let that happen. Not when he was stuck married to a Winthrop.

"That's enough!" Conn said. "Looks to me like someone just wanted to make trouble. Seems anybody bent on killing couldn't have missed from that distance."

They turned to look at the shaded area on the hill above the creek. It wasn't more than fifty yards away. What Conn said made sense.

"You all know Devlin Winthrop, my brother-in-law," Conn said, not above using Devlin's presence for his own purposes. "He and I are going to stand watch to make sure there are no more mishaps while you boys finish watering your cattle.

244

From now on, do your watering at different times of day."

"Aw, Conn," Eustis said.

"No arguments, Eustis. I've got as big a stake as anyone in seeing this truce succeed. Now get those cattle moved out of there."

Conn and Devlin sat on their horses, guns at the ready, until all the cattle had been watered and moved back out on the range to graze.

When the last of the cowboys had ridden away, Conn turned to Devlin. "I'd like to take a look up there in that stand of trees. Someone's bent on ending the truce. If he left some sign, I intend to find it. Want to join me?"

"Sure," Devlin said. "Let's go."

What the two men found baffled both of them.

"Look at this shell," Devlin said as he held it out to Conn. "It looks homemade. You ever seen anything like it?"

"Nope. Forty-five caliber, but the casings are a little odd. Nobody I know makes his own shells," Conn said, relieved to have evidence it wasn't Bentons who had fired the shots.

Devlin shook his head. "Looks damned suspicious to me. These shots were fired

245

by someone who has some very special skills. So who hired him?"

"Not Bentons," Conn said certainly.

"It wasn't Winthrops, either."

"It must have been one or the other," Conn said.

"Why?"

"Who else hates Winthrops or Bentons enough to kill them?" Conn said with a wry smile.

"Why does the killing have to be motivated by hate?" Devlin asked.

"What other reason is there to kill?"

"Greed."

Conn stared out over the valley before them, with the shining ribbon of water weaving through it. "You figure someone else wants this land? And plans to let us kill each other off so he can have it?"

"Something like that," Devlin agreed.

"You have someone particular in mind?"

Devlin pursed his lips. "There are some other ranches that could use this water. Bob Taylor's Bar T for one. Buck Simmons's Double B for another. Maybe they brought in some gunslinger to heat things up again."

Conn frowned. He had placed all the blame for the evils in his life on Winthrops, because they had been his mortal enemies.

But what if someone was playing each side off against the other for his own purposes? Conn felt a deep, searing anger at the thought that he, along with a lot of other people, had been so despicably manipulated.

He voiced the thought that was uppermost in his mind. "If it is someone outside the two families, we have to find him and put him out of business."

"Do we tell anyone else what we've found here?" Devlin asked.

Conn shook his head. "We've got enough people looking cross-eyed at each other. Maybe the two of us will just have to do some investigating on our own."

"You and me?" Devlin arched a disbelieving brow. "I thought you hated my guts."

"I do," Conn said. "But you've got a good head on your shoulders, so I might as well make use of it."

Devlin's lips curled in a rueful smile. "I'm willing. So long as you'll consider what I talked about this morning."

Conn eyed Devlin askance. "I'll think about it."

Beyond the next ridge a man lay on his belly and watched the two men on horseback dismount and search the area where he had so recently been. He had suspected they might come looking, so he had taken himself where he could watch in safety. He cursed the appearance of Conn Benton. Without him, things might have erupted into bloodshed. He wouldn't mind seeing Bentons and Winthrops die. He didn't even have to kill them himself; he had seen how willing they were to kill each other. He had failed on this occasion, but there would be others. He had plenty of time to do what had to be done. By the time that fool woman managed to get pregnant — if she ever did — he would have the feud back in full fury.

It was late when Emaline brought the clean sheets in from the line she found strung between two trees in back of the house and remade the bed. It was dark by the time she started supper, and she was busy making up excuses to Conn why she was so late getting food on the table.

She also took the time to clean herself up, to make herself pretty for Conn. She knew she was being foolish to think he would care one way or the other. But if there was any chance Conn could be attracted to her because of her looks, she wanted to take advantage of it. She put on a dress and combed her hair back, taming the worst of the curls. She patted on a dab of powder to moderate her freckles, and returned to the kitchen to await Conn's arrival.

It was two hours past sundown, and still he hadn't come.

She reminded herself that he had told her he would be home after dark. But Emaline felt a deep sense of foreboding. What if someone had decided to end the truce by killing Conn? What if he had made her pregnant last night and her child grew up without a father after all?

Because of the time he'd spent at the creek, Conn was later than he wanted to be completing the fence repairs. It was two hours past dark when he finished rubbing down his horse and headed for the kitchen door. He wondered if his new wife had waited supper on him. Probably not, he conceded. Better not to hope for it. Then he wouldn't be disappointed when he had to fend for himself.

Conn stood stunned at the kitchen door. There were candles and silverware on the table and the vase that had sat empty since his wife's death was filled with wildflowers.

He could smell something good cooking on the stove. But there wasn't a sound to be heard in the house. Where was Emaline?

Emaline knew she was being silly. But the later Conn was, the more she worried. And the more she worried, the angrier she got with Conn for making her worry. So when he called to her, she rose from the rocker in the bedroom like an avenging fury and strode out the bedroom door headed toward the kitchen.

She met him in the hall and stopped so abruptly that her calico skirt whirled around her. Her fingers folded into fists that were hidden in her skirt. "Where have you been?" she demanded. "It's been dark for hours!"

"I told you I'd be late," Conn said, keeping the edge from his voice. After all, he wasn't unmindful of the effort she'd gone to preparing supper.

"Late?" Emaline hissed. "I imagined you shot dead and buried." She backed him down the hall stabbing her finger in his chest. "You knew I would worry and —"

"How the hell would I know something like that?" Conn said. "I'm not used to answering to anyone, least of all a wife!"

"Well, so you finally remembered you have one," she snarled. "And decided to come home."

"And I'm damned sorry I did," Conn fired back as he stumbled backward across the threshold of the parlor. "If I'd known there was a shrew waiting for me —"

"Shrew!" Emaline shrieked. "I spent the day scrubbing and cleaning and cooking for you."

"Nobody asked you to do anything of the sort." Conn looked around and noticed the shine on the floor, the knickknacks on the piano and end tables, the extra pictures on the mantel. "What the hell is all this stuff doing here?" He gestured with a broad sweep of his hand.

Emaline stood in the parlor doorway, enraged at Conn's dismissal of her efforts, of her things, of *her*. "That *stuff* is mine! I live here, too, in case you've forgotten. I'm entitled to have a few of my own possessions around me."

"They don't belong in here. I liked this place the way it was." He quickly gathered a handful of items off the mantel and shoved them into her arms. "Get rid of this stuff."

Emaline marched past him and slammed everything back down exactly where it had been. "No! I've as much right to put things in here as you do."

"This house is mine!"

"And mine!" Emaline snapped back. "I'm your wife!"

"Much to my regret!"

"Oh, how I hate you!" Emaline said through gritted teeth. "When I think how I tried . . . What I hoped . . ."

"This was all your idea," Conn reminded her. He was having trouble keeping his hands off her. She looked magnificent with her blue eyes flashing, her back ramrod straight, thrusting her small breasts out at him. He wanted her, and she had given him the excuse he needed to take what he wanted. "There was only one reason I married you. And I intend to do what I promised to do."

Too late Emaline recognized the look in Conn's eyes. When had rage turned to desire? When had hate turned to passion? "No, Conn. Not now. Not like this."

"Right now. Like this."

When he reached for her, she ran. He caught her arm and yanked her around to face him. His arms closed tightly around her and his mouth came down hard on hers. They were both gasping when he lifted his head to stare down into her dazed eyes.

"You can fight me if you want, Emaline, but we both know that neither of us has any choice about this."

"You can't force me, Conn."

"I can, Emaline," he said in a harsh voice. "But it's not what I want. I'd rather have you willing."

"So you can tell yourself it's not rape?"

"As you've been so quick to remind me, you're my wife. I'm asking no more of you than what you promised when you married me."

"You know why I married you!"

"To bring peace through a child of ours," Conn said. "Are you saying you've changed your mind?"

Emaline bit her lower lip. Conn was wrong to demand she submit to him in this way, but submit to him she must, or else risk losing everything she had sacrificed to achieve. And though she had provoked him into showing his hand, she had learned something very important in their confrontation.

He desired her. It wasn't love, but it was a start.

Conn knew the moment she surrendered. Her body relaxed against his, her breasts pillowing against his chest, her hips slipping into the cradle of his. Her arms, which had been buckled between them, slid up around his neck.

"All right, Conn. You win. I'll couple with you."

He felt a stab of desire so swift and strong it nearly made him gasp. His hands cupped her buttocks and pulled her against him so she could feel his arousal. He looked down into blue eyes that were heavy lidded. She wanted him as much as he wanted her.

Conn lowered his mouth and claimed the woman in his arms.

Four

Emaline was pregnant. She hugged the knowledge to herself, unwilling to share it because they had been married for a mere six weeks, and it had occurred to her that once Conn knew, he would no longer have any reason to bed her. Emaline didn't want those interludes to end, because for those few hours she and Conn were as close as any two people could be.

It was only in bed that things were going so well. In their daily lives, toleration had grown to acceptance, but that was all. There were no signs of love between them. Yet.

But Emaline had done her level best to get to know Conn better and to help him get to know her.

On the first two Sundays of their marriage they had gone to dinner at the homes of their widowed parents, Clara Winthrop and Hester Benton. The exchange had been Emaline's idea. She had hoped to learn about Conn by getting to know his family and to help him get to know her better by spending some time with her mother and brother. It had seemed like a good idea at the time. It hadn't turned out exactly the way she planned.

Emaline had been appalled, when she and Conn arrived at her mother's one-story wooden house on the outskirts of town, to discover that the patriarch of the Winthrop clan, Jeremiah Winthrop, and his wife, Belle, had been invited as well. The tension that would ordinarily have existed at such a family gathering was multiplied tenfold.

She had felt the tautness in Conn's arm as he led her up the steps to greet her mother and brother on the shaded front porch. She had given her mother a hard hug and been squeezed breathless by her brother before she turned to include Conn in the welcome.

"Conn, you've met my mother, Clara, and my brother, Dev."

If Conn had been a real husband coming to call the first week after their marriage, he would have hugged her mother and heartily shaken her brother's hand. It was a sign of how different their relationship truly was that he tipped his hat to her mother and nodded curtly to her brother. That was when Jeremiah appeared in the doorway. Emaline could almost feel Conn's body recoil, though he didn't move an inch.

"How'd'do," Jeremiah said. He had a way of looking down his nose at people that should have seemed condescending, but the spectacles perched on the end of that protuberance gave him an excuse for his peculiar habit.

"I thought this was going to be a family dinner," Conn said.

"That it is," Jeremiah said with a smile. "Clara's my niece." Jeremiah reached out a hand to Conn. It was an offer of peace, an offer to let bygones be bygones.

Conn shot a startled look at Emaline before he slowly reached out to shake Jeremiah's hand once, then let it drop.

"Dinner's all ready," Clara said. "Shall we all go inside?" She was shooing everyone back inside, which was when Emaline saw Conn get another shock.

Her mother had an upright piano very similar to the one in his home, right down to the candlesticks and doilies on top. "You play?" he asked sharply.

She nodded. "Mother taught me."

"Why haven't you played for me?"

257

"I . . . I didn't think you wanted me to."

Conn grimaced. "It's foolish to let the thing sit there gathering dust. Feel free to use it whenever you like."

By then they had followed everyone to the dining room where Emaline found herself sitting on one side of Jeremiah, who was seated at the head of the table, while Conn sat across from her on Jeremiah's other side. Belle sat beside Conn and across from Devlin, while her mother sat at the far end of the table.

The table was already laden with food, and Emaline watched the dishes being passed as everyone served themselves. Conn had a confused look on his face as he ladled food onto his plate.

"What's the matter?" Emaline asked.

"What is this?"

"Cornmeal mush and black-eyed peas. It's a dish my grandmother used to make in Arkansas."

"I never had it before," Conn said flatly as he helped himself to several slices of ham.

"If you don't like it, you don't have to eat it." Emaline had trouble keeping the irritation out of her voice. It was rude to complain about what was served when you were a guest in someone else's house.

Conn's lips flattened grimly. "I didn't say I wouldn't eat it, only that I hadn't ever seen it before."

"Like I said —"

Her mother interrupted. "Shall we say grace now?"

Emaline watched to see whether Conn was going to participate. She saw him hesitate when he realized they were all joining hands, but then he took Jeremiah's and Belle's hands. To her surprise, he knew the grace and said it along with them.

She watched anxiously as he took a bite of mush and peas. He chewed slowly and swallowed. Then he reached for some butter and salt and applied both liberally before taking another bite. That one seemed to go down easier.

"Well, Conn," Jeremiah said, "I hope you've had a chance to realize what a wonderful woman you've married, even if you didn't exactly choose her for yourself."

Emaline nearly choked on her food. She spoke with her mouth full, not wanting to give Conn a chance to reply to such a personal, and potentially explosive, comment. "How's the roundup going, Dev?"

"Don't talk with your mouth full, Emaline," her mother chided.

Emaline flushed as Conn gave her a

ruefully sympathetic look. Apparently mothers were the same the world over.

"Things are going fine," Devlin said. "Only we're missing some cattle."

"Rustlers?" Conn asked with interest. That was something every ranch had to worry about.

"Maybe," Devlin replied. "Or maybe Bentons."

Conn's fork stopped in mid-air, and he lowered it with a clatter to his plate. "I didn't marry your sister so you could keep on making accusations like that."

"Boys, boys," Jeremiah soothed. "It's only been a week. I trust whatever happened in the past is in the past."

Emaline shot a pleading look at her brother. He relaxed in his chair. "Probably disappeared sometime during the winter," he conceded. "Got no way of knowing."

Conn started to make a retort, but Emaline caught his eye and gave him the same pleading look she had given her brother. Not that she expected it to work as well, but to her surprise, Conn picked up his fork and began eating again.

After that Clara and Jeremiah were careful to keep the conversation on neutral topics. When Clara offered dessert, Conn confessed to a full stomach and said he had chores to do anyway and that he and Emaline had to leave.

Emaline wasn't sure what she had accomplished with the dinner, aside from proving that Conn was still sensitive about his situation. On the way home he merely said, "Your mother's nice. She reminds me a lot of my own."

Dinner the following Sunday with Hester Benton was an enlightening experience for Emaline. In the first place, there were no men left in the family, just the widows of Conn's two brothers and their children. However, Horace Benton showed up. It didn't take Emaline long to figure out the Benton family patriarch was courting Hester. Horace was at least fifteen years older than Hester, but his hair showed only a few streaks of gray, and he had a toothsome smile that flashed often, giving him a youthful, almost mischievous appearance.

Emaline wondered how Conn could stand all the noise and commotion caused by the children who ran through the house whooping like Indians and slamming doors. He seemed totally oblivious as he sat talking animatedly with Melody and his other sister-in-law, Penny, who ran the milliner's shop in town. Emaline had never

261

seen Conn smile so much, never seen him so carefree. He looked so much younger and very handsome.

Hester came up beside her in the doorway to the parlor and stood with her watching the three of them talking together.

"Conn used to laugh all the time," she said. "But in the past two years it's been very hard for him. He loved Josie a great deal, and he was devastated by her death."

Emaline started to pull away, but Hester stopped her with a hand on her arm.

"I'm glad he married you," she said. "It's time for him to stop grieving and get on with his life."

"You don't hate the Winthrops?" Emaline asked.

Hester sighed. "I hated the feud and what it stole from all of us. You're a very courageous woman, Emaline."

"I didn't do anything —"

"Shucks, girl, you couldn't know you'd end up with a man as good as my Conn. But things'll be better now for everyone." She smiled. "And I'll have another grandchild to dandle on my knee."

Emaline flushed beet red. "Mrs. Benton —"

"Call me Hester," the older woman said.

"After all, we're family now."

Emaline watched with fascination at the supper table as Conn teased his mother about Horace's intentions. *So he doesn't mind that he's about to have a stepfather.*

She asked Conn about it on the way home. "I didn't realize your mother and Horace were sparking."

He managed a lazy grin. "She's been putting him off for a couple of years." The grin faded. "Maybe now that the feud's over she'll take him more seriously."

"The feud has interfered with all our lives more than we realize," Emaline murmured.

"Yeah," Conn agreed.

"I didn't know you liked children so much," Emaline said.

"What makes you think I do?"

She grinned, "You gave yourself away when you got into the pea-spitting contest with James. I thought Melody was going to take you both by the ears and lead you out to the woodshed."

Conn laughed. "I guess it shows, huh. Josie and I —"

He cut himself off, and that was the last he said on the subject. He would make a good father, she had realized. She and the child she would one day have were very lucky in that.

Emaline had no reason to feel particularly optimistic after those two dinners, but she did. Little things gave her hope. Like the fact that Conn kissed her good-bye each morning before he left. That he always came home before dark and made a point of complimenting her suppers. And that he joined her in the parlor after supper to sit by the fire and read while she worked on a sampler to hang in the kitchen.

Emaline knew he could just as easily have gone into his office in the back of the house to work and left her alone. He never said he enjoyed her company, he just spent time with her when he could. And their lovemaking had become the high point of her day.

Conn couldn't seem to get enough of touching her, caressing her, kissing her. He prolonged the moment when he would thrust inside her and spill his seed, so that by the time he did, she cried out from the pleasure he had given her. Then he would spoon her hips into his groin and slide an arm around her, bury his nose in the curls at her nape, and fall asleep.

Conn never spoke of his feelings, and she was too afraid to ask. Now those precious moments might be coming to an end, because he had accomplished what he had set out to do. She was expecting a child that should be born in time for Christmas, so the new year could truly begin with peace and goodwill toward all men.

She was going to have to tell Conn soon, unless she chose to pretend that her monthly courses had arrived on schedule.

Emaline bit her lower lip. Did she dare lie? Surely Conn wouldn't suspect anything for a month or two. And she could use the time she bought by her deceit to work on their relationship outside the bedroom.

Having made her decision, Emaline immediately put her plan into motion.

"Conn," she said that evening when they were sitting together in the parlor, "I wondered if we could go on a picnic this Saturday."

"What?"

"A picnic."

"I suppose so. If you'd like."

He had been secretly watching Emaline over the top of his newspaper, wondering whether enough time had passed for him to take her to bed. He had a hunger for her that made him ache all day. He could barely wait through the daylight hours until he could assuage it, then he wanted her again.

Conn blamed his obsession on the fact that they were constrained to couple nightly until Emaline was pregnant. Somehow, what should have been a burden had become such a source of pleasure that he couldn't imagine not loving Emaline at the end of the day. He thought about making love to her on Saturday under a tree somewhere, with the sunlight on her freckled skin. Would she be willing?

"I thought we could invite Devlin and Melody," Emaline said.

Conn frowned. He didn't like the idea of another couple joining them. He wasn't as opposed to the idea of Devlin and Melody getting married as he had been six weeks ago. Actually, he and Devlin had spent enough time together, breaking up altercations between Winthrops and Bentons, that he had learned to like and respect Emaline's brother. But he didn't completely trust him. Or any Winthrop.

Still that had nothing to do with his objection to having Devlin and Melody come along on their Saturday picnic. Frankly, if another couple joined them, they wouldn't have the privacy he needed to make love to Emaline. However, he wasn't willing to admit it. How he felt about Emaline was his own business. So he said, "You know

266

how I feel about the two of them."

Naturally, Emaline brushed away that excuse. "I think they make a lovely couple, and they're clearly in love." She set her sewing aside and crossed to kneel at Conn's feet, laying a hand on his thigh and looking up at him with beseeching blue eyes. "Say yes, Conn."

Conn was lost. "All right, Emaline. We'll go picnicking on Saturday. And I'll invite your brother when I see him tomorrow and ask him to bring Melody."

Conn dropped his newspaper beside the chair and lifted Emaline into his lap, tucking her head against his shoulder. She seemed willing enough to be there. Her hand slid up to his shoulder and around to his nape, where she played with his hair. A shiver of longing spiraled down his spine.

"Emaline," he said in a husky voice, "I want you."

"I want you, too, Conn," she murmured back.

He couldn't wait till bedtime. He lowered his mouth and kissed her as his hand closed over her breast.

Emaline moaned, and her hand tightened in Conn's hair, holding his mouth against her own as his tongue slid in and out, mimicking the love act.

It was the first time they had made love outside the bedroom since the second night of their marriage, when Conn had taken her in anger, and she had submitted in resentment. This was totally different. There was a willingness on both sides to please and to take pleasure. They were making love.

Conn shifted Emaline to the Turkish carpet that covered the parlor floor and lowered himself onto her. He was already aroused. He could hardly keep from ripping off buttons as he tugged Emaline's high-necked blouse from her skirt. Emaline was equally busy, eagerly unfastening Conn's shirt.

When Conn finally had Emaline naked to the waist, he stopped to admire her. Had he ever thought her freckles unattractive? He didn't now. He slid his fingertips across her ribs, across the silky flesh that always felt so good beneath his hand, then roamed upward to cup a breast and tease the nipple with his lips and tongue. Emaline arched upward, so incredibly responsive, so marvelously giving as he took more of her breast in his mouth and suckled her.

Emaline's hands caught in Conn's hair, and she held his mouth against her.

"Conn," she whispered. "Conn." She realized suddenly that she cared very deeply for this man who had been her enemy. But she didn't trust her feelings. Was it only this powerful physical attraction that drew them to each other? Was the taking and giving of pleasure all that existed between them? What did it mean to love? Was what she felt now love? Emaline had no answers, only the certain knowledge that it was no longer possible to face a future that didn't include Conn Benton.

When Conn had spilled his seed inside her, he carried her to the bedroom and made love to her again there. After he fell asleep, Emaline reached over to brush a stray curl from his forehead. Her heart ached with the knowledge that she was going to bear the child of a man who didn't love her. There had to be a way to make Conn realize that what they had found together was special, worth cherishing despite the circumstances that had united them.

Emaline kissed Conn good-bye the next morning as usual, then hitched up the wagon and drove herself the few miles to town. She had a visit to make to Doc Swilling. She knew she was pregnant, but she wanted to ask the doctor a few questions about childbearing that she couldn't ask any of the ladies of her acquaintance without giving away her delicate condition.

Doc Swilling confirmed that she could expect to bear Conn's child about the middle of December. He promised to let her make the announcement, but she could see from the beaming smile on his face that he was happy for her and for the town of Bitter Creek.

"You're about to put me out of work, Mrs. Benton," he said. "And high time, if you ask me!"

Emaline left Doc Swilling's office with a smile of her own, her step light. It was really happening. She was going to have a baby. She felt like grinning from ear to ear. She swung her reticule to let out some of the energy she felt. She was just passing an alley when she felt a hard hand grab hold of her arm and yank her into the darkness.

"Who —"

At first she thought it must be a thief intent on stealing her purse. She hadn't anything of value in it and would willingly have surrendered it, but she wasn't given the chance. An arm quickly closed around her neck, completely cutting off her air.

Emaline writhed to free herself and clutched at the restraining arm with both hands, clawing at it with her fingernails. She heard a grunt of pain, but her captor didn't lessen his hold. She panicked in earnest when the man — it had to be a man, he was so big and strong — covered her mouth and nose with his other hand.

Emaline felt faint and knew that if she didn't free herself quickly, she would die. And her baby would die with her. She wrenched her whole body in one gigantic effort to escape and almost won free. Almost. But not quite. She was nearly sobbing with fear and frustration as the villain tightened his hold once more.

"Hold still, or I'll kill you here and now."

Emaline froze. The man, whoever he was, had uncovered her nose at last. She took a deep breath, but she was so frightened she still felt suffocated. Her whole body was trembling.

"Why are you doing this?" she said behind his hand. It came out muffled, but intelligible.

"Bitch! It's disgusting how you spread your legs for a Benton. Murdering sons of bitches, all of them! Saw you coming from the doc's office. You got a Benton bastard planted in your belly yet? Answer me, girl!"

Emaline's throat was so constricted she couldn't get out any sound. Did he mean

271

to kill her? Would it make things worse if she admitted she was carrying Conn's child? She frantically shook her head no.

"I don't believe you," he spat. "Better to kill you now and not take the chance."

Emaline felt the man's grasp tightening and panicked. He was going to kill her. She was going to die without ever holding her child in her arms or having Conn look at her with love in his eyes.

Not without a fight, she wasn't.

Emaline was tall and strong. She started by lifting one well-shod foot and kicking backward at the man's kneecap. She heard him howl, and his grasp loosened around her mouth. She let out a bloodcurdling scream.

Immediately, faces appeared at the end of the alley. Her attacker must have realized he had no time to finish what he had started. A moment later, Emaline was free. She turned to see if she could identify the man, but all she saw was a fist flying toward her face. Before she could dodge, she felt a tremendous pain in her jaw, and she was rocked backward. Blackness closed in, and Emaline crumpled to the ground.

Conn hadn't realized just how much he cared for Emaline until a man from town had come riding hell-bent-for-leather to find him and told him that she was hurt and had been taken to Doc Swilling's office. He had thrown himself on his horse and galloped back to town.

She looked incredibly fragile lying on the iron cot in the doctor's office. Her face was pale and her eyes were closed. For a terrified moment he thought she was dead.

He sank down beside her on the cot. "Doc?"

"As far as I can tell, Conn, she just fainted," Doc Swilling said. "But she's had quite a scare. Apparently some man dragged her into the alley. She screamed, and some folks showed up and scared him away."

When Emaline opened her eyes, she was lying on an iron bed in Doc Swilling's office. She found herself staring into the eyes of a grim-faced man sitting beside her. It was Conn. She tried to smile but winced at the pain in her swollen jaw. "Hello, Conn," she whispered.

"What happened, Emaline?"

His voice was harsh, with no sympathy for what she had been through. Emaline began to tremble as she remembered how close she had come to being killed. As tears welled, she closed her eyes. "A man grabbed me when I was walking past the alley. He . . . he threatened to kill me."

Conn felt his heart turn over in his chest and realized he felt a great deal more for Emaline than he had ever admitted to himself. He pulled her into his arms, needing to feel the warmth of her, needing to know she was alive and that he hadn't lost her forever. He felt such a rush of rage and hate for the man who had threatened his wife that it made him tremble.

Conn was holding her so tightly that Emaline could barely breathe. "I'm fine, Conn," she said against his shoulder.

"You could have been killed. Who was it, Emaline? Who did it?"

She wasn't about to admit it was most likely a Winthrop. Who else hated Bentons so much? "I didn't get a look at him. It was too dark in the alley."

Either she truly didn't know, or she did know and wasn't saying, Conn thought. In any case, it wasn't hard to guess. It was someone who hated him or hated her for marrying him. It was the senseless feud beginning all over again. Bile rose in his throat, caused by a crawling fear of what might happen to Emaline.

"Can we go home now, Conn? Please?"

When Conn looked to Doc Swilling, he

said, "I've checked, and there's been no harm done to the baby."

Conn looked stunned. "Baby?"

"Why, yes. I just confirmed Mrs. Benton's suspicions this morning. The baby should arrive in time for Christmas."

Conn felt elation. And terror. Any threat to Emaline was now also a threat to their unborn child. His voice sounded amazingly calm to his ears as he said, "Then if it's all right with you, I'll take my wife home."

He lifted Emaline into his arms and carried her outside, where a crowd of people had gathered.

"Who did it, Conn?" one of the Bentons demanded.

"Who attacked her?" one of the Winthrops called.

A Winthrop shoved a Benton, who shoved back.

"Who you shovin' around?" the Winthrop shouted.

"A dirty, rotten Benton, that's who!"

The Benton man swung his fist. The Winthrop ducked, took two steps backward and laughed. "Missed!"

A second Benton turned on a second Winthrop and without warning slammed a fist into the man's jaw. "I didn't!" he said triumphantly.

There were a dozen Winthrops and Bentons gathered, and it looked as if a free-for-all was going to erupt right in the middle of Main Street.

Emaline could see that the truce was in serious danger. "Put me down, Conn," she said. "And see what you can do to stop that fight before it gets started. We've come too far to lose everything now."

Conn stared at her with a strange look in his eyes but did as she asked. He drew his gun and fired twice to get the attention of both Winthrops and Bentons.

"Emaline and I have an announcement to make," he said to the surly and sullen faces before him. "We're expecting our first child before Christmas."

There was a moment of profound silence before men who had been contemplating a fight with each other exchanged grins.

"Well, I'll be a pig in slop," said a Winthrop. "He did it!"

"Damn fast work, Conn," said a Benton, slapping Conn on the back.

Conn wasn't sure whether he felt more like blushing or grinning. He did both. At first, only Bentons congratulated him, but they were soon joined by the Winthrops, who shook his hand before tipping their hats to Emaline.

Winthrops and Bentons looked sheepishly at each other. Fighting no longer seemed like a very good idea.

"This calls for a drink!" a Benton said.

"More than one, if you ask me," a Winthrop replied. The crowd headed off toward the saloon. There were whoops and hollers of exultation along the street as they spread the news to anyone who would listen.

When they were gone, Conn turned back to Emaline, who was feeling light-headed again. "Conn, I think . . ."

He caught her as she started to fall and lifted her into his arms. "Let's go home, Emaline."

Once home, Conn put Emaline to bed and insisted she stay there. That evening, instead of making love to her, he merely pulled her into his arms and held her.

"You're in no shape to do anything but rest," Conn said. "Besides, there's no reason . . . now."

Emaline felt an ache in her chest. So, it was over, just as she had suspected it would be the moment Conn found out she was pregnant. At least he hadn't left her bed entirely. He was holding her lightly around the waist and her hips were spooned against his.

Conn's arms tightened around Emaline until he heard her moan slightly in her sleep. He loosened his grasp. He was terrified that he wouldn't be able to keep her safe. That some gunman would find her alone and kill her as Josie had been slain. Or that someone might sabotage the rigging on the wagon, and she would be thrown when the horses broke free. Or that she would be caught by some madman in an alley and strangled. He couldn't sleep for the visions that haunted him.

Now there would be a child by Christmas, an heir, to end the fighting forever, another life for which he was responsible.

Conn's hand slipped down to cover Emaline's abdomen. His son or daughter was growing inside her. He tried to remember how it had been with Josie. She had been four months pregnant when she was shot. Yes, there was just a tiny rounding of Emaline's belly now. His hands reached for her breasts. Were they tender yet? They seemed the same size as always, but he knew they would increase as the child grew inside her. Had she been sick? He hadn't seen any signs of it, though he believed it was common for women to

278

be ill in the first months.

His handling of her woke Emaline. "Conn?"

"Go back to sleep." He wanted to make love to her, but it was selfish to think only of himself. He knew her jaw was painfully bruised. And there was no reason for him to be loving her. She was already pregnant.

But when she turned to face him, he lowered his head and kissed her. And she kissed him back. He told himself he was just going to caress her shoulders to ease the tension there, but his hands roamed over her until at last he felt her hands on him. Another moment, and he knew he wouldn't be able to stop.

He grasped her shoulders and pushed her away. "Stop, Emaline."

He heard her cry of anguish and thought he must have hurt her. "Emaline? Are you all right?"

"I'm fine, Conn," she said in a quiet voice. "Go to sleep."

She didn't protest when he pulled her back into his arms. There might be no reason for making love, but there was nothing to keep him from holding her. Conn contented himself with the knowledge that when her jaw was well he could — and would — make love to her again.

★ ★ ★

By Saturday the bruise on Emaline's jaw had faded to a pale yellow, and she was insisting over Conn's protest that she felt well enough to go on the promised picnic with Melody and Devlin.

"I told Devlin yesterday when he came to visit that we're still going," Emaline said, "so they should be here any time. I've got everything packed and ready. There's no reason not to go."

Except there may be a gunman waiting in ambush to kill you, Conn thought. But he could see there was no persuading her to stay home. When Devlin arrived, he could see his brother-in-law felt as anxious as he did about the situation. But Emaline was insistent, and they gave in. The two men rode horseback, while the women took the spring wagon loaded with picnic supplies.

Devlin dropped back so he could speak with Conn without being overheard by the women. "I sure wish you could have talked Emmy out of this."

"I tried," Conn said. "She wouldn't budge. You know how stubborn she can be."

"I sure do!" Devlin said with a wry grin. "Have you found out any more about who attacked her?"

Conn shook his head. "All I can do is guess."

"I had such high hopes for this truce," Devlin said bleakly. "It seems all I've done the past six weeks is run around putting out little fires."

"Meanwhile, someone has started a blaze that we may not find until it's burning out of control," Conn said.

The women welcomed an opportunity to speak privately as much as the men had, but their discussion ran along a completely different track.

"I've been talking to Conn about your situation," Emaline said to Melody, "trying to convince him that he should consent to your marriage to Dev. I don't think he's as opposed to the idea as he was at first, but he insists on waiting a little longer to see if the truce lasts."

"What if it doesn't last?" Melody asked. "What happens to the two of you?"

"I'd never leave Conn for any reason."

"Why, you love him!"

"I think so," Emaline said with a shaky laugh. "I'm not sure what love is, but the feelings I have for Conn are different from anything I've ever felt before."

They picked a spot for the picnic along Bitter Creek not far from the house. The two men tethered their horses and helped the women down from the wagon. All four of them laid out blankets in the shade along with the picnic basket. Then they settled down to enjoy the sound of the creek rushing by and the wind in the cypress trees above them. As they ate, they talked about this and that, never broaching any subject that might cause friction among them . . . until Emaline turned to her brother and said, "You've never told me how you and Melody met."

Devlin shot a quick glance at Conn before he answered. "Not much to tell. I came upon a broken-down wagon a few miles outside of town. A woman and two little boys were trying to get the wheel back on. I stopped to help."

"And fell in love at first sight?" Emaline asked with a teasing grin.

Devlin laughed. "Hardly. The woman poked a gun in my chest and told me to leave her alone, that she'd sit there till doomsday before she took any help from me."

Melody flushed. "He was a Winthrop. I had reason to hate Winthrops."

Emaline watched as Melody and Devlin joined hands and gazed into each other's eyes. She began to realize they had conquered quite a few obstacles in coming to the understanding that now existed between them.

"So who held out the peace pipe?" Conn asked.

"I unbuckled my gunbelt and let it drop," Devlin said. "Then I told her she could keep the gun aimed at me as long as she felt she needed it, but I was going to fix that wheel for her. Otherwise she was going to end up stuck miles from town in the dark."

"After that incident," Melody continued, "it seemed we were constantly crossing paths in town. At first we just nodded to each other. Then we started saying hello. And then, one day I asked Dev to come to dinner, to repay him for the kindness of fixing that wheel."

"After the boys went to bed, we sat on the front porch and just talked," Devlin said. "It was as though we had known each other forever. Things developed pretty quickly after that. But there was nothing we could do. Not considering the feud, and all. Neither of our families would have allowed us to live in peace. Until now."

"When are you planning to get married?" Emaline asked.

Melody and Devlin exchanged glances,

then looked at Conn.

"What about sometime after Christmas?" Conn said.

Melody launched herself at Conn and gave him a hug. "Oh, thank you, Conn! Thank you!" Just as quickly she threw herself back into Devlin's open arms. "Oh, Dev, at last! At last!"

Emaline was happy for her brother, but envious as well, and uncomfortable with his vigorous demonstration of affection for his new fiancée. "Shall we go for a walk, Conn?" she suggested, extending her hand so he could help her to her feet.

Conn grinned wryly. "That sounds like a good idea." In fact, he planned to take advantage of the opportunity to act out his fantasy of having Emaline bared to the sunlight.

Emaline threaded her arm through Conn's, and they walked along the edge of the creek with the sun at their backs.

"I'm so pleased that you've agreed to let Melody marry my brother. I can't wait to help her plan the wedding."

"Just don't plan anything until after Christmas," Conn reminded her.

"Why not?"

"Because there's still a chance all of this could blow up in our faces. I don't want

Melody to become a target because she's hitched to someone on the wrong side when battle lines are drawn again."

"Do you really think things are as precarious as all that?"

"After what happened to you, I'm willing to believe anything. It's hard for everyone to change the habits of twenty years. I just don't want to take any chances."

Conn realized they had rounded a bend in the creek, and the other couple was out of sight. He turned Emaline toward him and cupped her face in his hands. "Have I told you how beautiful you look today with the sun shining on your face and the wind blowing in your hair?"

Emaline couldn't believe what she was hearing. It actually sounded like the sort of thing a beau might say to his sweetheart when he was courting her. In fact, the way Conn was looking at her, she no longer felt like an ugly duckling. He made of her a gracious swan.

"Am I beautiful, Conn?"

"You are to me, Emaline."

She lifted her mouth as he lowered his, and their lips clung. It was a moment of recognition that there was more between them than the forced vows they had taken on their wedding day. If only the rest of the

285

world would let them live in peace.

Conn leaned his forehead against Emaline's. "I want to make love to you here by the creek with the sunlight overhead and the grass beneath us. That's why I wanted to come alone today, Emaline," he confessed.

"We're alone now, Conn," she said in a soft voice.

"Would you be willing?"

She was already unbuttoning her shirtwaist. She grinned as she met his dark eyes. "Oh, yes, Conn. I definitely would."

There, with the sun streaming through the trees overhead, and the creek burbling alongside them, Conn made love to his wife. He had never laughed so much or felt such heights of passion as he did that day with the cool grass beneath their naked bodies and the sunlight on her freckled skin. He was ready to love her. He wanted to love her.

And yet, he could not love her. Not yet. It was simply too dangerous to give his heart to her. He couldn't survive another tragedy like the last one. It would destroy him to lose another wife, another child. So he made love to her with his body, cherished her with his mouth and hands, but he kept his soul to himself.

Emaline knew what Conn had given her and what he had not. It was more than she had let herself hope for. Maybe he didn't love her as wholly, as completely, as she loved him. But they had the rest of their lives together. Anything could happen.

Five

Emaline was heavy with child. She spent her days sewing clothes for the baby and playing every Christmas carol she could remember on the piano. She had insisted that she and Conn have a tree, and he had gone into the mountains to cut one. They had decorated it with ornaments they had made together out of pine cones, juniper berries and the lids cut from tinned food. They had also arranged candles around the tree to provide light at night. As she stood with Conn and admired their efforts, Emaline felt the baby move inside her.

"Feel, Conn," she said as she reached for his hand and laid it on her swollen girth. She could visibly see a hand or foot moving beneath her flesh. "He wants to be here to celebrate with us."

"He's a week late already. If he doesn't hurry, he's going to miss Christmas altogether," Conn said.

"He's still got another week to go," she replied.

Conn circled Emaline from behind, weaving his hands together over her abdomen so he could feel the restless child moving inside her. "What makes you think it's a boy?" he asked.

"It might be a girl," she said. "I'd be happy with either one. I just want our child, boy or girl, to be able to live in peace."

"That's what this marriage is all about," Conn said quietly. He paused and added, "Are you sorry, Emaline?"

"Sorry? For what?"

"For having married me."

She relaxed back into his embrace. "No, I'm not sorry, Conn. I'd do it again." *I love you, Conn,* she thought. But she didn't say the words aloud. She was waiting for him to say them first.

"Are you happy about the baby?"

"You know I am. Because it will bring peace at last." *And because it's a part of you and me.* But she didn't tell him that, either. She wasn't willing to speak before Conn made his feelings known. She felt too vulnerable. She couldn't take the chance that he didn't share her feelings.

Conn said nothing more, just turned her toward the bedroom and followed her there.

He had watched Emaline pray for peace each night and marveled at her faith in mankind. There wasn't going to be any peace he thought cynically. At the last minute something would happen to spoil it all. He could feel it in his gut.

And yet it was impossible to ignore the child growing inside her day by day, week by week, month by month. He had felt it kick. He had seen it move beneath her flesh. He had listened for the sound of its heartbeat in her womb. He knew it was alive, that it was real. But until he held it in his arms, he refused to let himself believe that everything would turn out all right. He kept waiting for the other shoe to drop.

Overnight, Emaline became convinced that something was wrong with the baby. It was already a week overdue, and there were no signs that it was coming anytime soon. She didn't want to worry Conn, but she needed some reassurance that everything was all right. The instant he left the house the next morning, she headed for town in the spring wagon to see Doc Swilling.

"There's nothing wrong," the doctor assured her after his examination. "Babies simply have a habit of coming when they're good and ready."

"But I'm ready now," Emaline said with a grimace. She could no longer see her feet. Getting up and down without assistance was impossible. And she was tired of having to make so many visits to the john. She wanted this done and over with. She wanted to hold her child in her arms. She wanted Conn to believe that it was all right to love her. She wanted peace at last.

The summer and autumn had passed without any incidents of violence between Winthrops and Bentons that resulted in death. There were, however, several unexplained "accidents." The well was fouled at Tom Benton's ranch by a dead chicken. Winthrop cattle ended up in a pasture full of crazyweed and a bunch got sick and died. Wolf poison was laid too near Zeb Winthrop's barn and his prize hunting hounds ate it and died. And someone shot at a wagonload of Bentons on their way home from church. One of the horses was killed and had to be cut from the traces.

In the past, such incidents would have called for some sort of retaliation against the other side. Even if the exact perpetrator remained unknown, they knew who to blame for the crime. But no human beings had been harmed. For the sake of the truce, both Bentons and

Winthrops let the incidents remain unre-
solved and unrevenged.

Instead, new, peaceful habits were being
formed. With the impending birth of a
child who would possess the blood of both
sides, and thus secure the disputed water
rights to Winthrops and Bentons alike,
hope was growing that the killing feud
might be over at last.

It was bitterly cold outside. A blue
norther had recently swept through,
leaving behind a dusting of snow and drifts
along the fence lines. All day Conn had
been trying to talk Emaline out of at-
tending the Grange Christmas social. "It's
too cold outside, Emaline," he argued.
"You'll catch a chill riding all the way into
town. And what if your labor starts?"

"I'll bundle up warmly, Conn. And if my
labor starts, we won't have to send for the
doctor, because Doc Swilling will be right
there. I'm as strong as a horse. I'll be fine.
Besides, I want to dance."

Conn took one look at his wife's bulk
and laughed out loud. "I'll be lucky if I can
get my arms around you!"

"Then I'll find someone who can!"

Conn caught her arm and whirled her
into his embrace. He wasn't far off the

mark. His arms barely made it around her girth to close behind her. "All right," he conceded. "We'll go to the dance. But you're going to rest between numbers. And we're coming home early."

Emaline readily agreed to Conn's conditions. She hadn't planned to dance a great deal anyway. Mostly she wanted a chance to visit with Melody and talk with the ladies present about the impending birth of her child. The immense size of her belly made the idea of giving birth a little daunting. She feared the pain and wanted some reassurance that she could manage it.

As Conn drove Emaline into town in the wagon, his eyes constantly shifted to cover the horizon. He hadn't forgotten, even if she had, that someone had tried to kill her in the spring. The culprit had never been found, and Conn knew he was out there somewhere waiting for another opportunity to finish what he had started. Conn had guarded Emaline well over the past months, never letting her travel without an escort, always making sure she had someone with her in town. She had chafed at the constraints he put on her but had conceded that there was just cause for his concern.

He wondered what he would do if he ever caught the man responsible for attacking his wife. Shoot him and risk starting the feud all over again? Turn him over for trial by a jury of his peers? Hell, if he was a Winthrop a jury of Winthrops would just let him go again.

"What are you thinking?" Emaline asked when she saw the furrows of worry on Conn's brow.

"I'm thinking it'll be a long time before Bentons and Winthrops ever learn to trust each other."

"I trust you. Melody trusts Devlin."

"That's not trust, it's love," Conn said.

"You have to trust first, before love can grow."

"Oh, is that how it is?"

"That's how it is."

It took a moment for Conn to realize that Emaline was suggesting her love for him had grown once she had learned to trust him. On some level he had known for a long time that she loved him. She had never said the words, but then, neither had he. He wasn't sure what she was waiting for. Plain old fear was stopping him.

Several weeks ago he had taken the daguerreotype of himself and Josie from the piano, where it had been since the day

Josie had died, and carried it into his office. He had sat for a long time staring at it with eyes that eventually blurred with tears. He had never grieved for Josie, he realized. He had been too consumed by hate. Now, two years later, he felt an ache in his chest, and there was a painful lump in his throat. He had fought the tears that threatened, but couldn't hold back a choking sob. He pressed the heels of his hands against his eyes as anguish dammed for years gushed over a wall that had somehow come tumbling down.

Conn wasn't sure when he first realized Emaline had come into the room, but he turned to her and buried his face against her growing belly and cried for what had been lost. She had closed her arms around him and stroked his hair and murmured words of comfort that he understood even though he never heard them.

When he had fallen silent again, he had been embarrassed because she had seen him like that. But Emaline had brushed aside his apologies.

"You loved her, Conn," she had said. "You should grieve that she's gone."

He had captured her mouth, grateful for her understanding, seeking solace for the pain, and discovered something unexpected in her arms. The emptiness, the place that had become a void when Josie died, had been filled again. He didn't have to face life alone. He had Emaline.

He had put the daguerreotype in his desk drawer for safekeeping. It was no longer necessary to remind himself every day of his pain, to nurture his hatred of Winthrops. He was going to have to stop hating if there was to be any future for himself and Emaline. And their child.

His thoughts were brought to a halt when they pulled up at the barn where the dance was being held.

"Hey, you two! We've been waiting for you," Devlin called. "What took you so long?" Devlin had his arm around Melody, and he let go of her to help Emaline from the wagon. Before he could touch her, Conn was at her side, his hands at her waist.

"I've got her," he told Devlin.

They could hear the music coming from the barn. A couple of violins and a piano could make a lot of ruckus, Conn thought. He could see that Emaline's toes were already tapping.

"Come on, wife," he said, slipping an arm around her and leading her toward the noise. "Let's go kick up our heels."

Emaline eyed the green and red wreaths strung across the ceiling as Conn whirled her in the dance. She was so dizzy from looking up that she felt breathless, yet she had a smile on her face that spread from ear to ear. It was wonderful dancing with Conn. It was wonderful looking around the room and seeing faces that were smiling instead of sullen with suspicion.

Emaline's happiness fueled the hatred of the man who had attacked her in the spring until his heart pounded in his chest, and he felt dizzy. Christmas was awful for him this year, because he was alone. But they all seemed happy. Especially her. His heavy fists opened and closed, as he yearned to close them around the flesh at her throat. Nor should the child in her belly be allowed to live. Because his child had died. Emaline had become a symbol of all he despised, and he would know no peace until she was dead.

No guns had been allowed in the barn for obvious reasons, but he had hidden a pistol in his coat pocket. He didn't care what happened to him, as long as Emaline Benton died before he did.

He was aware of the music only as a raucous noise in his head, aware of the people around him only as sources of heat and movement, aware of the lanterns hung around the barn only as a sort of burning radiance, guiding his way to vengeance. His eyes were focused on her as he crossed the barn. At last he would be free of the pain. He would kill it when he killed the woman.

Conn couldn't take his eyes off Emaline's face. He had never seen her so happy. She seemed to glow with warmth. He felt a swelling of love in his breast so strong it made him want to shout. But Conn did nothing more than smile himself, a small tilting of his lips that did little to reveal the upheaval inside. Because he was watching her, he saw the growing uncertainty on Emaline's face, followed by a dawning horror.

"Emaline? What's wrong?"

He followed her gaze and felt his heart skip a beat. John Fleet, the blacksmith who had lost his daughter in the stampede, was pointing a gun at Emaline.

"It's all your fault," Fleet said in a voice loud enough to garner attention from the dancers nearby. "And now you have to pay."

When the gun in Fleet's hand became

visible, the dancers edged backward out of harm's way. Until only the three of them, Conn and Emaline and John Fleet, stood in a corner of the barn.

The musicians abruptly stopped playing. In the sudden silence, the frozen Bentons and Winthrops could easily hear what was being said.

"My little girl is dead because of Bentons and Winthrops," Fleet continued. "And now you want them to stop fighting." He shook his head. "They have to keep killing each other off, until they're all gone. That's the only way my little girl will ever have any peace, if all of them, every last Benton and Winthrop, is dead. I tried to get them to fight. I shot at some. And pulled down fences. And poisoned wells. And killed their dogs. But they wouldn't fight.

"So you see, I have to kill you. And the baby. Because you want peace, and I can't have that." He turned to Conn, standing no more than a foot from Emaline. "Get out of the way, Conn. I only want her."

Conn shook his head. A muscle in his jaw jerked. "I won't let you do this, Fleet. I can't let you do it. She's my wife. I love her."

There were several gasps at Conn's declaration of love for a Winthrop woman. They all knew how he had hated Winthrops when he married her. And there wasn't a man or woman in the room who didn't wonder just how far his love would take him. Would a Benton give his life for a Winthrop?

A bleak look appeared on Fleet's face. "I don't have any choice, Conn." He cocked the gun and pointed it at Emaline's heart. "It has to be done."

"I love you, Conn," Emaline said, fearing that if she didn't speak she would never have the chance. Their gazes locked and suddenly Emaline realized what Conn planned to do. "No, Conn!"

He had less than a second to act. At the same instant that Fleet fired, Conn launched himself toward Emaline. The bullet caught him in the back as he fell with her, doing his best to lessen the effect of his fall on her pregnant body. Once they were down, his body sagged against her.

At the same time that Conn threw himself at Emaline, Devlin drove his shoulder into Fleet's belly and shoved him off his feet. The gun went flying. Moments later, Bentons and Winthrops alike had gathered to subdue the blacksmith. The sheriff was summoned to take him to jail.

Bentons and Winthrops stared at each other with new eyes. Clearly each side had been innocent of the incidents over the summer that had raised so much furor. If that was true, maybe both sides did want peace. They had seen how a Benton had offered his own life to save a Winthrop. And how Devlin Winthrop had leapt forward to help a couple of Bentons. Maybe it was time to let go of the past and look forward to the future.

Everyone crowded around Conn until Doc Swilling had to yell, "Get back and give me some room to work."

Emaline sat on the floor, cradling Conn's head on her lap. "Please don't die, Conn," she whispered in his ear. "Please don't die."

"How is he?" Devlin asked as he crouched beside his sister.

"If someone would give me some room to see, maybe I could tell you," Doc Swilling replied irritably.

Devlin moved the crowd back until they stood in a wide circle around Conn and Emaline. With the space he needed, Doc Swilling examined Conn and announced, "Didn't hit any vital organs, but that bullet has to come out."

"Will he be all right?" Emaline asked.

"His chances are good," he said. He turned to the crowd. "A couple of you carry him over to my office."

Bentons hurried to do the doc's bidding and found themselves facing Winthrops on the other side. By mutual agreement both Winthrops and Bentons shared the labor of carrying Conn down the street to the doc's office.

Emaline followed after them, Devlin on one side supporting her and Melody on the other. Emaline felt the first pain as she set foot outside the barn. It was just a twinge really, but she had learned enough to recognize it as the beginning of her labor.

She refused to leave Conn's side while the doctor performed surgery. "If he dies, I want to be with him."

The surgery didn't take long, but Emaline was grateful that Conn remained unconscious throughout it. Once he had been bandaged, Doc Swilling took one look at her pale, sweat-bedaubed face and said, "You need some rest, young lady."

Emaline smiled. "I'm afraid I'm not going to be getting much rest for the next few hours, Doc." She laid a hand on her belly. "This baby has decided to be born."

There was a furor among those waiting

for news of Conn when they heard Emaline was in labor. Doc asked for another bed to be brought to his office and several hardy souls retrieved one from the boardinghouse.

"Are you sure you wouldn't rather go somewhere else to have this baby?" Doc Swilling asked.

"I want to stay with Conn."

Doc Swilling directed the men to set the second bed a foot away from the first and as soon as they were gone, relegated Emaline to it. "I don't want to see a toe on the floor, young lady, until that baby is delivered."

Devlin and Melody were allowed in to see Emaline, but Doc Swilling's office wasn't large enough for them to stay long, especially with the two beds crowded so close together.

Emaline had wished for a mercifully short labor, but her body didn't cooperate. She had been in labor for eight hours when Conn finally awoke. She turned on her side to face him. "Good morning."

"It's still dark out," he replied in a raspy voice.

"It'll be dawn soon."

There was a pause before he asked, "Where are we?"

"In Doc Swilling's office. They brought in an extra bed for me."

"You should have gone home, Emaline," Conn chided.

"I didn't want to leave you. Besides, I needed to be close to Doc Swilling, too."

He tried to rise and fell back with a groan. "You were shot, too? Are you all right? Is the baby —"

"I wasn't shot," Emaline said, reaching out a hand to grasp Conn's. "It's the baby. It finally decided to come."

A stunned look appeared on Conn's face. "You're in labor?"

Emaline nodded. Then she gasped and bit her lip. Her hand clenched around Conn's. "Just . . . having a . . . contraction . . . now," she said panting.

Conn used his stomach muscles to get himself into an upright position and managed to place his feet on the floor. But he was dizzy and his back and shoulder hurt abominably. A lantern had been left burning on a table near the beds. Conn looked around and realized they were alone.

"Where the hell is Doc Swilling?" he demanded.

"He went upstairs to get some sleep. He said it would be hours before I need him, but if I did to yell for him."

"Why didn't you yell?" Conn demanded when he saw how tired and pale she was.

"Because I don't need him."

Conn shifted from his bed to sit on the side of hers. "You're in pain," he said, brushing damp curls from her forehead.

"That's the general idea in labor," Emaline said with a hard-won smile. "It won't be much longer," she reassured him. She hoped she was right. The pains were much closer now, and longer, and she was having greater difficulty not crying out. She grasped Conn's hand again and squeezed hard as another contraction rolled over her, absorbing her, wracking her body with excruciating pain.

"Emaline!" Conn said. "Is there anything I can do to help?"

She didn't answer until the contraction was finished. Then she took a shaky breath. "Just knowing you're here helps."

He leaned over to brush her forehead with a kiss. "I was afraid I was going to lose you, Emaline. I couldn't have borne that."

"I love you, Conn. I wish I'd said it sooner. I've felt it for a long time."

"And I love you, Emaline. I was just afraid . . ."

"I know, Conn. But I think tonight was a turning point for all of us. Poor Mr. Fleet. He must have gone crazy when his daughter was killed. But his confession means that Winthrops and Bentons really have managed to get through all these months without attacking each other. Maybe everyone is willing to change for the better. Maybe there will be peace at —"

Emaline gasped as another contraction caught her in mid-sentence.

"Should this be happening again so soon?" Conn asked as Emaline grasped his hand with enough strength to crush it. How did women bear such pain? he wondered.

"Conn," Emaline said a moment later. "Call the doctor."

"Emaline? What's wrong?"

"Call the doctor," she insisted.

"Swilling!" Conn yelled at the top of his voice. "Get the hell down here where you belong!"

Conn heard the doctor's shout of acknowledgement and then the sound of footsteps on the stairs. A moment later, the rumpled physician appeared.

"There's something wrong," Conn said anxiously. "Help her, Doc!"

Conn shifted back to his own bed while

the doctor examined Emaline. "Is she going to be all right?"

"Right as rain," Swilling pronounced. "But this baby is on its way."

Conn wished for a moment that he was somewhere else, anywhere else, and didn't have to go through this with Emaline. It hurt him to see her in pain. But there was nothing he could do for her. She had to bear the child alone.

A guttural sound forced its way past Emaline's lips. "I — have — to — push," she said through gritted teeth.

"Then by all means push," Doc Swilling said.

"It — hurts," Emaline said in a grating voice.

"I'm here, Emaline," Conn said, grasping her hand.

"Go — away — Conn." But even as she said the words she tightened her hold on his hand.

"Push, Emaline," Conn said. "Keep pushing."

"I see the head. It won't be long, Emaline."

Emaline panted as she waited for the next contraction. "Do you want a girl, or a boy, Conn? You've never said."

"I'd like a son," Conn confessed. "But a

daughter would be nice, too, Emaline."

Conn felt her tense as another contraction began. She raised her shoulders and bore down. "Conn!" she cried.

He watched, amazed, as the child slid out of her body and into the doctor's waiting hands.

"It's a boy!" the doctor said.

The baby let out a wail at the indignity of being forced out of his warm haven into the cold world. Once the cord was cut, Doc Swilling wrapped him in a blanket he had ready and placed him in Emaline's arms. When the birthing was done, the doctor rinsed his hands and rolled down his sleeves before getting his coat from the rack near the door. "I'll just go spread the news and leave you two alone for a little while." He left his office, quietly closing the door behind him.

Emaline met Conn's misted gaze and smiled. "It's a boy, Conn. A son."

"Thank you, Emaline," he said in a husky voice. He leaned over and pressed his lips to hers. "Thank you so very much."

"What shall we call him?"

"I haven't thought about a name."

"How about . . . Winthrop Benton?" she suggested.

"It fits," Conn said with a wry grin. "He's half one and half the other. It'll help remind people that we have a stake in getting along."

Emaline moved the blanket aside so she could see her son's face. "Well, Winthrop Benton, welcome to Bitter Creek."

Emaline had barely finished speaking when the first visitors came barging through the door in a rush. It was her mother with Jeremiah and Belle, followed closely by Dev and Melody. Dev was carrying a small Christmas tree on a wooden base, which he stood in the corner of the doctor's office.

"Wasn't sure when you and Conn would get out of here, Emmy, and I didn't want you two to miss Christmas," Dev said as he bent to kiss his sister, meanwhile getting a good look at the new baby. "Hey, the kid has your red hair!"

"But no freckles, thank God," Emaline said with a grin.

"I want to see my grandchild." Clara reached to take the baby from Emaline's arms. She held it so Jeremiah and Belle could see. "Isn't he the most precious thing you've ever seen?"

"He's got the Winthrop eyes, all right," Jeremiah said. "Blue as a cornflower."

A swirl of cold air blew in as Conn's mother arrived with Horace. "Conn? Are you all right?" she asked anxiously.

"I'm fine, Ma."

"Brought a gift for the baby," Horace said, offering Conn a package.

"Why don't you give it to Emaline?"

Horace turned and handed the package over. "Just a little something for the tyke."

Emaline opened the package and found a beautiful christening gown. "Thank you, Horace."

"Hester made it," Horace said, winking and grinning broadly.

"Thank you, Hester," Emaline said. "It's lovely."

"You'll be wanting to see this child," Clara said as she handed the baby over to its other grandmother.

Hester opened the blanket and stood with tears in her eyes, looking down at the child, Horace at her shoulder. "He's so beautiful," she said in an awed voice. "His mouth and chin are the same as Conn's when he was a baby."

"He's a Benton, all right," Horace said.

"He's more Winthrop than Benton," Jeremiah retorted. "Got the Winthrop hair and eyes."

"Got a Benton nose," Horace argued.

"He's both!" Emaline said with asperity. She reached out. "May I have Win back?"

"Is that his name?" Hester asked.

"It's Winthrop Benton," Conn said. "After *both* families."

Jeremiah looked down his nose at Horace. Horace grinned back. "Winthrop Benton it is!"

By now Doc Swilling's news had made it up one side of Main Street and down the other. More knocks came at the door as Bentons and Winthrops began to arrive. They crowded inside with gifts for the child, which they placed beneath the tree Dev had brought. The room was soon filled to overflowing with signs of Christmas cheer.

Emaline reached for Conn's hand and held it as they gazed into each other's eyes. There was no need for words. A child had been born on a cold winter's night. And like that other child, who had been born so many years ago, he would bring peace, at last, to this tiny bit of earth.

Christmas had come to Bitter Creek.

About the Author

One of the most popular romance writers in America today, former attorney and college professor **Joan Johnston**, a *New York Times* bestseller, has over 10 million books in print worldwide.